AF408996

TAKE ME

CHAPTER 1

"Darla? Did you hear me?"

"Yah."

"-is coming from the airport around four. We have him at the Newport, presidential suite. Dinner at seven. Hope that's not too late?" The assistant continued while Darla stared into the East coast horizon.

Sighing inwardly so Marilyn wouldn't know of her dissatisfaction, Darla continued to stare at the blue sky of heaven kissing white sands below, known as Miami. People would give their eye-teeth to live here. Have this job. Be her.

Be her.

How did I get here? She pondered. I gave more than my eye-teeth, that's for sure. How can I have come so far, yet still have such discontent? I have everything. Everything!

Well, almost.

"How's that?"

"Hmm?" Darla answered, her eyes refocusing.

Marilyn pushed her glasses up along her nose and sighed. "Okay, how much should I repeat?" She felt for her boss. Marilyn would never desire the immense stress of being a CEO, but she truly had an incredible life with Darla as her boss. She wouldn't give it up for anything. Marilyn couldn't pinpoint what Darla's distraction was all about these last few months, but her melancholy was palpable. Not yet costly for the company, but worrisome, none the less.

Darla raised her hand to stop Marilyn's flipping back through pages of scheduling regarding the last 17 minutes of unappreciated soliloquy. She noted the perky breasts that every 20-something-year- old boasted, pointing through her crisp white professional blouse. So firm and taunt. Darla winced at the frustration of her 40-year-old breasts resembling a three-dimensional pancake.

"We're good?"

Good. Are we good? Am I good? Her thoughts drifted.

The memory of her father asking her the same thing while her mother lay limp and fading as the hospice nurse busied herself packing supplies before she left for the night, filled her current state of mind.

"Yes, Daddy. We're good. I can stay the night. You need your rest." She had sat by her mother's side and held her fragile, unresponsive hand. Not too much longer, the nurse had told them.

Just two days before, mother and daughter lay cuddled together on the chaise lounge laughing and ribbing each other about girl stuff, before her morphine kicked in, causing hours of drowsy, dulled sleep. Now, short puffs of labored breathing, the mouth slightly opened, eyelids still and closed, signaled the change of conscious life to that of one slipping away to ethereal freedom.

Her dad's voice trailing to the kitchen reminded her of why she needed **her** freedom.

"We need more meat in this house. Who's going to go to the grocery store? Any idea on when you're going to get married? Your mom wanted to see you in her dress. It might be too late…" His voice trailed off, muffled by the refrigerator door holding his colossal frame while he peered in, denial clouding his reality.

Cold rebellion rose without restraint in her answer. He knew the answer to both questions, perhaps unsure about the why. "Because I'm a vagitarian!" With tension in her voice, she spoke the words with steeled edge, aware that her words could easily be misconstrued.

Darla looked down at her mother's flaccid form. She thought for a brief instant she saw a smirk of delight in the curve of her mouth for goading the old man. Because her mother knew the truth of who she was and who she loved and loved her for it, anyway. Praised her for her glorious, worthy soul, and courageous choices. Until she was ready, she would keep her secret from her father, a 32 year Air Force veteran. But no. No jesting smile, just the shadows play from the west-facing open window, whose light competed with the floating curtain lifting with the breeze.

"What?!"

She spoke louder. "I'm a vegetarian, Daddy. You know that." She added silently to herself, *for the most part. No more men either.*

"Yes. I suppose I do." He looked glumly again into the depth of the cold shelves, hoping somehow he had missed a piece of chicken, a steak, or, God forbid, even a hotdog.

He closed the door with the sadness of a lost friend and joined Darla in the bedroom. He sighed heavily as he sat beside her and pulled his only daughter into a side embrace and frowned at the lessened form that called true as the love of his life.

"She was such a good wife." His voice faltered. "An amazing mother to you." With the only support he knew how, he added as a compliment, "You both are so good. Such good women." He squeezed her tight.

Good. Yes, I'm good. Aren't I? Never the son you wanted, but I'm good. Good enough. For now.

"Earth! Earth, to Darla. Come in please!"

She wrenched her attention back to the present. "Yep! Got it. Analytical stats for the new bottle design going to

Marsha today, Mr. Torres in at 4, dinner at 7 and tomorrow meeting with him regarding the final three scents for the Bella Diaz campaign at the Genia Gardens with a luncheon at Islandia." Darla proceeded to walk toward Marilyn signaling an exit of her office and the day. "I guess I'm the entertainment committee."

"For the 1.2 million dollar investment he's bringing, you might aspire to be more than that."

"Gross! I didn't get here sleeping my way to the top."

"Amen to that. But, I've seen this guy. I'd sleep with him no matter which direction I was going."

Darla looked sideways at her assistant as they walked. Her eyes widened with surprise at this sudden confession.

"And so it would be only logical as your assistant," she continued, "if I accompanied you two to the luncheon tomorrow, on the boat, with champagne, maybe not getting in until, oh I don't know, after the sun sets?" Marilyn pleaded her case with her youthful puppy dog like pouting request written upon her face.

"Absolutely not! You'd be too much of a distraction. We're here to make money, not babies."

"Have you seen this guy? Even you'd want to get pregnant." She laughed.

Darla *humphed*. "Speaking of fantasies, did we get a lock on the new Canadian account for Fantasy, teen scents?"

"Working on it. Speaking of *that*, Gayle called. Three times." She handed her boss the messages.

"Why speaking of fantasies?"

"Because, if you're so inclined to remember, Gayle is the one that introduced you to the Fantasy management team in Canada. A year ago," she added with emphasis, "today." Marilyn pressed the button of the private elevator door to rise to the executive suite.

"Oh God! Our anniversary. I totally forgot."

"No, you didn't. You sent Stargazer lilies to her when she was with her pinochle group this afternoon simply signed XO. There's champagne and chocolates arriving at her townhouse in the limo. Ohhh," she looked at her watch, "right about now. And, you're meeting her for hors-d'oeuvres at the Mo Bar & Lounge in 10 minutes. Get a move on."

"I-."

"Have the teal satin dress with crystal high heels in the corporate car along with a silver and sapphire bracelet for Gayle, complete with a bow. Now get going!"

Darla smiled a big smile. As she turned in the elevator she said, grinning, "You sure you're not gay?" She giggled. "I could hook you up."

"Nope! Like me a penis. Any size, any shape." Marilyn lifted the corners of her mouth in a smirk, as she looked her boss up and down from the firm, athletic calves, slim hips, and heart-shaped face with hazel eyes accentuated with long lashes to the small mouth with pert lips. She cocked her head and raised her eyebrows and said simply, "Tempting."

Darla looked appreciatively at her assistant and dear friend of nine years, who more than earned her three figure salary. She brought two fingers to her lips in a kiss and pointed them back at Marilyn just as the doors closed.

CHAPTER 2

One-year anniversary. The sigh came again unexpectedly. Darla knew Gayle was a magnificent woman. Worldly, well educated, filthy rich, older, mature, seasoned. No games. They met in Seattle at a CEO conference where they both spoke about gender acceptance and human resource training for strategies in the workforce. Those to be embraced, not changed.

Over the years they shared a few cocktails, hours of phone conversation, daily emails, and then Gayle moved to a condo in Miami. Darla held to her executive suite amidst pleas from Gayle to move in. It went beyond simply not being prepared. She loved Gayle, liked her, and respected her. She was not sure she was **in** love with her. Besides, Darla's contract with the Miami team would be up in just three more months, and then what? Head hunters were already approaching her to accept the next contract; Rome, the Netherlands,

Australia. Companies eager to have her at the helm to improve their brand, making them the next billion dollar company.

She smiled at the thought of her girlfriend. Gayle brought a sense of tranquility to Darla's life. She created moments of safety and warmth. The physical intimacy they shared was gentle and familiar, like the taste of vanilla. Gayle's infectious laughter created a buoyant atmosphere of kindness. Darla cherished the rare relief of finding someone who could engage in deep conversations late into the night, without imposing any demands on her. However, the equilibrium they had wasn't necessarily fair. At least not to Gayle.

Darla read her phone messages from earlier today as she made her way to the car. The first one simply said 'call me', the second, 'thank you darling, for the beautiful flowers,' the third a reminder, 'don't forget I have symphony tonight.'

Well, she had forgotten, and felt a little guilty. This would give her the out to leave the dinner early tonight, with Torres, without having to apologize, but still give Gayle the attention she deserved. She winced. Shouldn't it feel more natural?

Her driver opened her door for her to enter and pulled quickly from the curb while she closed the darkened privacy window. Just as Marilyn said, a satin teal dress, complete with accessories, awaited her transformation for a lovely celebration with her partner.

"When do you think you'll get married? ... your mother's dress..."

As the corporate car arrived at Mo's, Darla peeked in the gift box so she wouldn't look more surprised herself when Gayle opened it. *Tacky.* She deserves more than this. She tried to still the dark pit in her stomach.

Darla remembered her traveler's work contract and thought how often she used work as an excuse to untangle herself from relationships, from love, from *nice*.

She heard Gayle's laughter the moment she entered the lounge. Looking inquisitively through the foliage that decorated the entrance, she saw Gayle and three of her friends, well, their friends, at a table, overstuffed chairs, a love seat, and drinks in hand. Not sure if she felt perturbed or relieved, Darla made a swift entrance, complete with a bright smile.

"Darling! We were just talking about you!" Gayle rose and quick kissed Darla's cheeks. "Come! Sit." She waved at the bartender, who moved with light agility, placing a tall glass on the bar, already known to mix a double gimlet for the latest arrival. "You remember Beth, Alexa, Trina." She pointed to each one as they responded with a smile and a nod, grabbing a glass to sip, stilling whatever previous gossip they were dipping into.

"I do! So good of you to join us on our anniversary." Darla said with a noted loss of composure.

"Oh Darling, you don't mind do you? Fun always follows when the girls are around!"

With a relief, the drink arrived. Darla responded sincerely, "Of course not. Always glad to have our friends about. Tell me. What have you all been up to?"

The hours flew by quickly, and Darla felt more than tipsy. She was not sure she could regain her sense of control before the 7:00 dinner which was in…, "Oh God! Gayle, I have to go. I'm going to be late."

"You made plans for tonight?"

"No! Well, I mean yes. You know I despise the symphony, right? So, I have a short meeting with a client, since I knew you were going out," she lied. "I didn't want to sit home alone. Let's meet up later. Home, a club? What do you want?" She prayed this diversion would cover her forgetting their anniversary, altogether.

Gayle blew cigarette smoke through her smile as she ground out the filtered stub. She looked up at Darla. "How about tomorrow? Just the two of us. At the beach?" Her eyes narrowed, unconvinced of Darla's sincerity.

Darla felt that pit in her stomach grow even bigger as she replied, "I'd love to, really, but this new client. It's a big deal and we're going to the gardens to sample fragrances."

"Well! I guess it's home then. When should I expect you?"

Darla paused, realizing she hadn't planned for this moment. Nonetheless, with a convenient excuse to go home, she could escape from Torres earlier than expected. She knew it would be a painfully dull meeting, filled with tedious conversations about achievements, statistics, and perhaps even some flirting on his part if he believed it would lead to something. Just in case the deal didn't go well, he would have a memorable conquest to boast about. Typical.

"Let's say 10:00. Deal?"

Gayle laughed that musical laugh of hers and said, "Make it eleven. I have our friends to drop off after symphony."

Darla felt startled. She wasn't even aware that Gayle attended these galas with friends. She always believed it was a solitary event.

"Deal?" Gayle added curtly.

Embarrassed, Darla realized she was still standing, poised to leave. "Here, I bought you something for this evening." She handed the ribboned box to Gayle. Darla's cheeks crimsoned in frustration.

Gayle responded softer, as she unwrapped the little square box, "Thank you. So kind." She gave a quick gasp of approval and her friends joined in with gleeful ooh's and ah's and clapping. "Here!" She raised the box to Darla with the expectation of assistance for putting it on. Gayle turned her left wrist ever so slightly one way then the other, after placement of the bauble, so the dimmed lights could catch the twinkle of sapphire against sterling. If Gayle felt the jewelry was duplicitous in nature, she did not show it.

"Love you, my dear." Darla leaned over the sofa and kissed her cheek.

"And I as well. This!" She pointed at her wrist, "So nice." Her smile was big.

Nice.

CHAPTER 3

She had 20 minutes to make a 40 minute drive. Darla hated being late. It was a rule for her to arrive shortly after a client. Let them get settled first. But not impatient. Not a good move to be notably late.

If a man is late, they take it in stride. Blame the weather, blame the traffic. If a woman is late, she's ditzy, unmotivated, unorganized, no matter the reason.

Darla changed back into her French-cut white chiffon blouse and light gray pencil skirt, pairing them with taupe nylons. Her charcoal pumps, with a closed toe and heel measuring three and a half inches, had an elegant tweed inlay. Opting for a more modest look, she decided to forgo any jewelry. She swept her shoulder-length ash-colored hair back and secured it in a twist, choosing not to reapply her lipstick. As she contemplated her tardiness, she realized she didn't want to compensate by appearing overly polished with makeup, fearing it would make her seem like she was trying too hard, something she had been doing a lot of lately, with everyone.

1.2 million dollars. Get it together.

When the driver pulled up to the Newport, she told him to take the rest of the night off. She would call a taxi to return. It would tell the client she was not expecting him to return home with her or that she had a flashy car to flaunt. It would appear frugal. Men liked that in a woman.

Slowly and with purposeful confidence, she walked into the hotel and made her way to DeMarco's restaurant. The time was 7:20 pm.

Darla swiftly scoured the room for an impatient, high maintenance, self-deluded client that felt entitled to have her there at his beck and call. He would be the one checking his watch, with an empty glass or two in front of him from drinking too much or typing furiously on his phone, making the next deal of a lifetime, which might not have her name on it.

Her second glance brought her back to a lone figure in a bright, white silk shirt, open at the chest and khaki trousers. He was leaning back in his chair with his arm casually draped over the chair beside him. The large brown eyes were gentle and matched the soft smile that he laid upon her gaze. He looked neither frustrated, impatient nor eager.

Darla was confused.

As she approached, he arose and pulled out the chair opposite him and gestured for her to sit. Which she did. When he reached out his hand and said, "Miss Weston." her mouth slightly parted in hesitation.

"It is so good to meet you, Mr. Torres."

He placed a hand over hers and firmly clasped her hands and said, "Please, call me Drey."

"Drey. I'm…well you know who I am. Of course." *What the hell is the matter with me?* "Mr. Torres-."

She glanced down at his gesture, appearing almost hypnotized. His tanned skin was soft and his hands lean, but firm. He released the grip and stepped behind her to push in her chair, leaning just so very slightly in, he brushed the side of her hair with his shoulder. As she raised her head to thank him, she caught the essence of his smell.

She felt loopy. Is this guy wearing pheromones? *That bastard.*

"I hope you don't mind I took the liberty of ordering sparkling cider and smoked oysters for us."

Darla gulped her water. She had to get this gimlet buzz under control. When what he had said finally sank in, she felt startled. "That's exactly what I would have ordered."

"We don't get good oysters in Teresina like you do here. It's a treat."

"That's where you're from? In Brazil?"

"Yes. The state of Piaui. It's quite beautiful."

She listened to him talk of his country, his culture, his love of perfumes and the creation of unfamiliar scents that he aspired to have immortalized like Chanel, Dior, and Calvin Klein. She smiled at his candor of who he was in his community, his ideas, and marveled how he could be so in touch with the feminine without being overbearing and pretentious. His voice was soft, with just a touch of gravel. When he looked at her and smiled, there was a glimmer of something. What was it? Gentle confidence. But, something more. The thought evaporated as the food arrived.

Her knowledge of curing and processing flowers and plants for scent impressed him. They talked of the history of fragrance and how it affects us worldwide, from every generation to every culture. Her head cleared by the fourth oyster and second glass of sparkling cider. So much for my diet.

"What are you wearing by the way? It's intoxicating."

"You like it?"

Again that warm smile and Latino tan. It was stirring her loins, and she felt mildly uncomfortable. No wonder Marilyn wanted this guy to impregnate her. She simply nodded her head and slurped another oyster.

"It's my personal creation. I have not marketed it yet. It has my own pheromones and a few special blends of vanilla and salt I produce in Teresina. I hope to take you there some day."

Darla jerked her head up, while choking on the tabasco, as she could not swallow with that last comment. *Oh no. This deal is going to sour because I'm a lesbian.*

"I think you have me-. "

"Oh look! Our main course. Paella. I hope you like it."

"I didn't realize they had Paella on the menu."

"They don't. I brought it with me." He tucked a large starchy cloth napkin in his shirt. "Well, that is, my chef did."

"Your chef did?" With wonder, she examined the Paella on her plate and glanced at his face, questioning his seriousness. "They let you, put your chef in their kitchen? To make Paella?"

"Mhmm. And a wonderful kitchen staff it is too. I'm so glad you recommended this hotel." She watched him eat heartily as the spicy, flavorful

rice and chicken with chorizo and
shrimp filled his mouth over and over.

"Mmm, Mmm, Mmm." He dabbed at
the juice escaping the corner of his
mouth. "You hardly ate a thing. Aren't
you hungry? You're just kinda eating
around your plate there."

*Discombobulated. That's what I am.
Too much meat.* "Stuffed to the gills!"
She said, aloud.

He waved a half raised hand and
within seconds a to-go box appeared.
"Take this home. We have a big day
tomorrow. We should get some rest."

He was leading the way. Had been
the whole evening. Her calculations to
coerce him to be on her team seemed
mute. Before she knew it, they were
outside of the hotel.

"I'll just walk you to your car. But,
Darla?"

"Yes?" She braced herself.

"I understand you have a boat rented for us to go out to Islandia for lunch tomorrow."

"Is there somewhere else you would rather go? I can change-."

"No! That would be great. I prefer to go by helicopter instead. There's something else I want you to see."

"You brought your own helicopter pilot as well?" She laughed.

His face was solemn. He wasn't joking.

"I'd be happy to. I'll see you in the morning then."

"Where's your driver?" He looked around with curiosity.

"I'm taking a cab," she said, smiling in triumph.

"Oh. I thought you had a company vehicle. More practical."

Damn it!

He held out an empty arm that only suggested a touch and smiled warmly. "See you tomorrow then."

The taxi ride was endless. Her disappointment burned hot in her cheeks. No strategy she employed tonight brought about the cunning results she had hoped for. When she finally did reach her suite, she hastily packed an overnight bag and a fresh casual suit and flats for tomorrow's outing. The next taxi ride was shorter and far more relaxing as Darla looked forward to making up for her insensitive, 2nd hand arrangements of the evening with Gayle.

Her key slipped easily in the lock and she entered the dimly lit entry. The maid would be gone for the evening by now. Darla brought in her bags, surprised she had not heard Gayle call out her usual greeting. As Darla placed her keys on the corner table and removed her shoes, she realized with

disappointment hers were the only
accessories present.

Gayle was still out with their friends.

CHAPTER 4

With the fluidity of a panther on the prowl, Darla glided towards the lush greenhouse garden. The anticipation bubbling in her stomach felt like a kaleidoscope of butterflies, fluttering with excitement for this new creative endeavor. The contracts awaiting her were the essence of her success, and she savored the thrill of immersing herself in unfamiliar trades, gathering extraordinary knowledge, and wholeheartedly educating herself on the company's vision. This time, the funds for launching a fragrance empire, supported by international investors, would infuse a Latin country influence, cleverly marketed in America. It embodied the epitome of true corporate finesse.

Her wide-legged silk SoHo trousers swayed with a gentle rustling sound as she walked, the fabric brushing against her legs. Darla pushed her oversized glasses up to the top of her head, feeling

the cool touch of the frames against her
temples. As she did so, the length of her
ash-colored hair cascaded forward,
caressing her cheeks.

She felt a modest sense of elegance
in her mid-waist lace top; the satin loops
forming delicate daisy patterns, adding a
touch of femininity. It was a garment
that invited stares, with its angular
design accentuating her graceful
appearance. The soft fabric clung to her
skin, creating a subtle sensation of
comfort, in addition to chic style.

With her arms toned and slightly sun-
kissed from a summer filled with
boating and beach outings with Gayle,
she exuded a carefree lifestyle. Her toe
nails, painted in a dusty rose color after
a recent Pedi-cure, peeked through her
hot pink wedge sandals with every step
she took.

But it was her attitude that truly
caught people off guard. With a
confident stride and a piercing gaze, she

left clients unexpectedly taken aback. The sound of her heels clicking on the polished floor echoed throughout the room, commanding attention. The faint scent of her signature perfume lingered in the air, adding to her aura of authority. Those who initially judged her appearance as someone with her head in the clouds soon realized their mistake. Darla was not someone to be underestimated–she could chew gum and walk at the same time, effortlessly multitasking with precision and grace.

God, I love being a woman, she thought, as the sunlight caressed her skin, casting a warm glow on her face. The gentle breeze whispered through her hair, carrying the scent of blooming flowers. Men just don't know what they're missing, she mused, the laughter of other staff, echoing in the background. Or maybe they just don't know what they have when they're with a woman. With a pang in her heart, she conjured a vivid image of Gayle, their shared moments flooding her mind, making her realize that perhaps her own misgivings were intertwined with love's complex dance.

"Miss Weston? This way."

She looked at the Latino attendant, assuming he was part of Torres' staff. How pretentious, she thought. He always does whatever he wants, just like any typical male asserting his power. He led her into the covered garden area exclusively for their scent sampling session. Excitement surged through her. The attendant took her handbag and glasses, then handed her a lab coat. The coat's large pockets contained goggles on one side and a notepad with a pen on the other.

She smiled with amusement, her lips curving upwards as she saw him swiftly pivot at the sound of her melodic voice. Through the lenses of her goggles and behind the protective face mask she donned, he appeared somewhat diminished, overshadowed by the pristine whiteness of his lab coat. His wide grin illuminated his face, radiating joy in a dazzling display. With an exuberant wave, Drey's hand danced through the air. As she drew closer, her happiness was almost palpable, infusing the air with an enchanting aura.

Respectfully, she stood by his side and absorbed the local curator's words as the instructor educated them about the distillation process of a unique orchid species from Hawaii. Seamlessly, they moved between the various lab stations with diligence, jotting down notes regarding the scents they had mixed and matched. Pleasant smiles accompanied some explanations and approving nods, while others brought frowns and disapproving head shakes. However, they both agreed on the presence of tones that were already too familiar in the market. Each of them selected a personal favorite blend, as well as a few combinations that they believed aligned with the marketing plan. The company would further test these choices in the laboratory to determine their popularity.

"Miss?" A white-jacketed waiter with white gloves handed Darla a tall, misty, glassed drink.

"Lemonade with lime juice." Drey said, with a twinkle in his eye. Taking a glass of the refreshment himself, he guided them to a table to relax and re-charge.

"My favorite!" With appreciation, she took a long swill of the iced, refreshing beverage. Her sigh was clear relief. Drey studied the moisture beading on her upper lip.

"In my country, the sights, and sounds of nature are a part of us. Our day, our mood, even our ability to complete daily tasks are part of nature's response." The flow of his accent was intoxicating, and Darla found herself drifting.

Unintentionally, or perhaps out of curiosity, Darla's gaze wandered towards his subtly exposed body. His unbuttoned silk shirt showcased a golden chest, devoid of hair. The snugness of his nylon slacks accentuated the contours of his muscular thighs, while his perfectly sculpted backside seemed like an ass only a God should have.

Stop! Check impulses. Yep. They're out of control.

"Are you wearing that perfume again?"

"You mean mine? The one I personally made? Yes. You like it?"

She took a quick sip of her drink to mask the flush rising to her face.

With amusement at her discomfort, he smiled. "What do you think I should call it?"

"Heart Attack."

Laughing, he said, "I want you to put some on. Let's see what it does to me."

"No way!" she exclaimed, her voice filled with disbelief. But deep down, curiosity stirred within her. She couldn't help but wonder how it would smell on her, how it would envelop her senses. Closing her eyes, she envisioned the scene unfolding before her.

She imagined the gentle touch of his fingers, gliding the fragrance along the delicate curve of her jawline. The soft sound of the bottle rolling against her skin echoed in her mind. As it reached the hollow of her sternum, a shiver ran down her spine, anticipation building within her.

Her imagination took her further, to the intimate space between her breasts. She could almost feel the warmth of his breath, his mouth and nose brushing against her quivering skin. In that moment, she envisioned him inhaling her essence, the sweet aroma mingling with the air around them.

The scene played out in her mind, each sensory detail vivid and enticing. The sights, sounds, smells, and feelings merged together, creating a tantalizing experience that left her longing for more.

"What do you say to that?"

Her eyes widened in surprise, and she instinctively slammed her hand onto the table, trying to ground herself in reality. She hadn't heard a single word he had said.

Sensing her confusion, he stood up and spoke with genuine concern in his voice. "You look pale. Let's go grab some lunch." As he prepared to pull her chair away from the table, he leaned in once more, brushing his innocent lips against her ear.

She simply nodded, her knees feeling weak, as if they could give way at any moment. What was it about Drey that had such a hold on her? She struggled to regain her composure as she caught the faint sound of helicopter blades in the distance, signaling their imminent departure. Darla knew she was in for the adventure of a lifetime.

CHAPTER 5

The ride through the air was spectacular. Pods of dolphins dotted the waves as they flew along. Their plunging, rising art form accentuated the path to Islandia, a small island on the Elliot Key. They spoke very little, seemingly at peace with their surroundings as they traveled to their relaxing location for a scrumptious lunch of roasted quinoa and pine nuts, three cheese and spinach quiche followed by caramel flan.

Darla felt at ease and quite satisfied that she didn't have to pretend to enjoy being with this client or struggle for entertainment.

"A quick walk on the beach?"

"Sure! Is this what you wanted to show me?"

"No," Drey responded. "That's on the way home."

Spontaneously, they both took off their shoes and welcomed the warm, gritty sand on the soles of their feet as they walked with no purpose other than to feel the texture between the sand line and the water's edge. The smell of salt water and fresh air was intoxicating, and Darla found herself smiling with a sense of feeling carefree. A strong breeze lifted her sun hat from her head.

He lunged forward and caught it, handing it back to her, tugging it back as she grabbed it from him. "Can I ask you a question?"

"Sure!" she said, unguarded.

"You are so well traveled, long successful career, multi-leveled education, and scads of friends. How come you're not married?"

"The million dollar question, I get regularly from my dad."

She looked pensively ahead as they walked. A sand dollar hidden in a drift of sand caught her eye and she picked it up, caressing the rough edges before putting it in her pocket as a souvenir.

"I haven't found my match. I've looked. Been close a few times. Somehow it always seems like making a commitment means making a sacrifice." She thought of her mother. "I just don't want to go there." Darla stole a sideways glance toward him, awaiting his judgement. "Sounds vain. Doesn't it?"

He was throwing bits of driftwood into the air to land on mounds of the white and beige granules. "No. Not at all."

"Are you looking to be married?"

"Oh, yes!" He said with a hopeful air. He looked at her, expecting her gaze of interest, but she remained with eyes focused forward.

"I have a type in mind." He continued. "Maybe that is my misgiving.

But, I won't sacrifice that. I'd rather be alone."

"Type?" she said with curiosity. The wind wound up between them again, causing friction to the mood.

He sighed. "This woman, my wife, my soulmate. We are equals. I listen to her. I respect her. Perhaps we are in the same line of business or she has her own creative endeavors. She is a powerhouse, intelligent, thoughtful. Our time together is playful, tender … enduring. We have each other, and that is everything."

Darla turned her head as though the water's rising white caps interested her. She furtively wiped away a tear. *If only you were a woman.*

Without notice, a sudden gust of rain brought looming clouds in its wake and he grabbed her hand. They dashed to a rocky ledge where he pulled off his windbreaker and covered her as he laughed with glee. His amusement tickled her, and she relaxed despite their physical closeness.

The storm's gloom was brief and just as suddenly as it came, the sun broke through grey veiled clouds and restored balance to the mood.

They walked to the helicopter readjusting their footing both literally and figuratively.

As the helicopter gracefully ascended into the sky, changing its course towards the southern part of the key, she couldn't contain her curiosity any longer. Looking at him with a sparkle in her eyes, she playfully questioned, "Okay, mystery man. Where are we going?"

His smile was big. "The Rockland Hammock just outside of Key West."

Her disappointed frown and furrowed brow drew more laughter from him.

"This is a unique place that serves as a habitat for 40 endangered species of animals, including the Schaus, and at least 60 rare and protected plants." He looked expectantly at her.

"The what?" She asked dully.

"A rare swallowtail butterfly! Come on!" He elbowed her to elicit interest. "You're going love it."

Her pursed lips in a maybe seemed a disappointment for him. But, she conceded mentally, this was out of her comfort zone and she probably needed it.

And, as usual, he was right. The afternoon was a whirlwind of amazing sights and sounds. Colors splashed across the landscape like an artist's palette. Animal and vegetation blended with such subtlety that it was hard to tell one from the other.

Just before they entered the helicopter for the final leg of the afternoon, the ranger came by with a wounded key deer. Darla watched as Drey lowered himself to ground level to assess the animal. She marveled at his strong masculinity but gentleness and compassion with the animal as she stood beside him. She noted his soft, curly brown hair and light side burns with no facial hair or stubble. His wiry, lean body without too much muscle made her loins ache. *Safety*. He is short at 5'9," instead of the overbearing nature of a 6'1"man like her father, which is intimidating and always has been, she noted.

I'm not changing.

His mood was exuberant. Hers, dour. Drey ignored her grumpiness and misunderstood her trembling as a result of the cool air pouring through the overhead vent. He presented her with a cream and cobalt blue Alpaca fringed wrap he had bought specifically for her.

He tried unsuccessfully to place it around her shoulders.

Darla snatched it from him and said too brusquely, "I'm a Lesbian!"

He stalled his movement and stared at her. "I know."

"You know?"

"Mhmm."

"I'm not going to change!"

"I hope to God you don't."

With a snap in her voice she asked, "What else do you think you know about me?"

"That you play at being a vegetarian. That you graduated summa com laude as one of the youngest of your class, that you snagged a top assistant job with Louie Vuitton and started your career with merchandise campaigns as one of the most sought after CEO developers in the world within five years, and that you only pretended to like my paella."

She winced.

He continued with confidence. "That you love sunflowers and hate the cold and that your mother died four months ago and you probably haven't properly grieved for her yet."

A feeling of threat replaced shock and surprise with that last revelation. She showered him with resentment.

"I hate it that you know so much about me. Why? Why am I so important to you?"

"Well, I hate it that you don't know *anything* about me and that you never ask about how I feel or what I want!"

"Why would I?" she snapped.

Softly, but firmly, he spoke, "Why wouldn't you? I can feel it." He whispered the last sentence and leaned in towards her. "I know how I affect you. I want you to want me." He kept her focus on him with his mesmerizing intensity. "I've been watching your climb to success for years. We're alike you and me. I know you're favorite music, you're favorite drinks, what movies you like. That your love language is receiving gifts but giving, is physical touch –."

"Stop!!! You have no right. How dare you! What business is it of yours to know me so intimately? I tell you who I am and you just ignore it-."

His voice roared back at her. "I tell you what I want and you just rebuke me. You're not even willing to explore this!"

"THIS? There is no, this!"

Unbeknownst to her,. the helicopter had landed, its propellers gradually slowing. As the attendant opened the door, she seized the opportunity and swiftly escaped to the waiting driver.

CHAPTER 6

Sex with Gayle that night was fierce. Darla entered the condo with the door slamming behind her. Startled, Gayle came out of the kitchen to the foyer with a slice of avocado toast in one hand, a martini in the other.

Darla's face was dark with intensity as she pushed Gayle's arms forcefully up and over her head, causing her body to collide with the wall. The avocado toast lay securely stuck to the wall while the martini glass crashed to the floor, creating a sharp shattering sound. A whimper escaped Gayle's lips.

Darla pushed her body into the softness between Gayle's legs and bumped her chin to the right, leaving her throat exposed. With a sense of possession, Darla brought Gayle's warm skin into her mouth and bit down.

"Ouch!!" Gayle resounded, a mixture of shock and slight displeasure evident in her voice. Ignoring the response,

Darla released Gayle's arms and griped the back of her head, pulling her fiercely into her mouth, demanding rather than requesting. She bit again, this time drawing blood.

"Darla! You're hurting me!" She cried sharply, but not with delight.

Darla drew back. Her breath in deep heaves. Sweat dripped from her temples and her body quivered in the deepest anticipation. "I'm sorry. I'm so sorry," she repeated. Gently, but with purpose, she swiveled Gayle to the winding staircase and laid her gently on the last three steps. She pulled open Gayle's blouse with little finesse. While she sucked hungrily at her breast, her fingers found Gayle's sweet spot and she rubbed through the slickness around her clit.

Gayle allowed her fingers to enter Darla's throbbing pussy, instantly feeling the rolling shudder of her partner's first orgasm.

Darla's deep moan was only briefly interrupted by her mouth moving to Gayle's other breast, her face nuzzling deep into her pillowed softness. In a frenzy, she continued to rub Gayle, only aware of the rising pleasure within her own body escalating to a fevered pitch.

Gayle slid three fingers upward to palm Darla's clit. Soft slow rubs, were interspersed with a split of her fingers that then clasped and pulled at Darla's hardened cherry until with a forceful cry, Darla came again, so long and so hard, when she finally quieted, she fell back in exhaustion, utterly spent.

Her quickened breath once again under control, Darla looked over at Gayle and said with disappointment, "You didn't come."

Gayle only shook her head. Her gaze bore into Darla as though she saw only a stranger before her.

Fatigued, Darla spoke hoarsely, "I'm sorry I hurt you."

"It's not even the pain. I don't know who you were making love to but, it wasn't me."

*   *   *

The long weekend ended with a sense of emptiness. Quiet corners, silent walls. Gayle left for work Monday morning with a wave and a slight smile. Not the jovial, bright soul she usually emanated.

Darla felt sullen on her drive to the office, stopping briefly at a Starbucks for a bagel and a caramel macchiato. Going through the motions of preparing for the workday, she barely noticed they had arrived at work until her driver broke through her stupor.

Several hours passed, filled with phone calls, emails, and a never-ending list of tasks. Darla sat in her office chair, swaying slightly as she contemplated her next move, the taste of ink lingering on her tongue.

When Marilyn entered, her brow furrowed with concern. "Last task!" She stated.

A vibrant array of colored photographs, neatly stacked, adorned the table before them. The air carried the faint scent of ink and paper, while the soft click of markers being uncapped resonated in the quiet room. Bottle designs occupied their thoughts as they prepared to end the workday.

Darla nodded. They worked side by side, without conversation. The work partners traded stacks and marked the same ones for consideration, tossing the ones they knew were not the standard Hewitt expected, so in synch were they from years of working together.

Finally, Darla got up, stretching and placed the much reduced stack of black and white photos for final consideration on the 'to do', pile for tomorrow. She selected a short stack of slogan lines in various types of prints.

Marilyn noted the cashmere wrap that lay along the back of Darla's office chair with surprise. "That's Lucchese!" She exclaimed. Emphasizing each next word, she said, "Where- did- you- get- that?"

"Drey," she half whispered. Her eyes fell on the shawl and looked dreamily at the soft pattern. "Well, I suppose it's time to head home."

"Mmm. You know you need to break that off right? It's just not going anywhere."

"What?" Darla looked sad. "I'm not starting anything with him, it's just …"

"Him? Wow! I wasn't even thinking along those lines. I was talking about Gayle. You and Gayle."

Darla looked up with shock. Not only was Marilyn right about her and Gayle, but surprisingly to her as well, as this conversation revealed, she did have thoughts of a relationship with Drey. Undercurrents not yet vocalized, but torrentially unexpressed, nonetheless.

"I hate to do it, but you're right. I'll probably run off to the Netherlands for my next contract. I wouldn't feel honest asking her to go with me. It's bad enough I have you living out of a suitcase."

"Well that's my choice. But I just mean you and Gayle … seem like the best of friends. Right?"

"She's a beautiful woman."

"But not passionate and fiery like Drey. Am I right?"

"I'm not interested in him like that."

"So you say."

If only you were a woman.

The memory of him holding his coat over them, leaning into her and enveloping her with his smell. The body warmth. The rain. The painful argument. *I can't give up who I am.*

Marilyn's voice pierced her thoughts. "I just wonder if you avoid relationships so you don't have to tell your dad you're a lesbian, then you can somewhat honestly say you just haven't found the right one yet."

"Okay, Freud." They continued silently to process campaign slogans for some time.

Marilyn couldn't hold it in. "He owns that animal sanctuary in the Keys."

Darla looked at Marilyn with shock flooding her face. I really don't know anything about him, she thought.

"That's why he took you there. Not to show off, but to probably see if you were a compassionate human being." She leaned back in her chair with a sigh. "Sometimes I think you're an alien. There's gotta be more to work and

the next million dollar conquest rolling
around in there somewhere. Isn't there?"

Chapter 7

As soon as Darla stepped into their home, her attention was immediately drawn to the sound of Gayle's excited voice. Hearing Darla come in, Gayle appeared from the other room, cradling a fluffy puppy in her arms.

"A puppy? Honestly, Gayle," Darla exclaimed, her voice tinged with frustration.

"I just thought you would like some company for the nights you stay at your place. You know," Gayle said. Her voice filled with hope. "Besides, you went against my advice and ripped up that beautiful bedroom carpet. A dog would be perfect to potty train there."

Again with the carpet. Last month Darla had a perfectly good Berber carpet taken out of her bedroom to luxuriate in the wooden floor beneath it. Gayle felt it would be harder to keep clean with the dust and just downright ugly. Darla argued and went ahead with what she wanted.

Now, Darla's expression remained cool and unappreciative. She thought to herself, I barely make time for relationships, how can I take the time to train a puppy?

Frustration clearly grew etched across Gayle's face. She handed the puppy over to the maid, the disappointment palpable. The couple retreated to the living room; tension lingering in the air.

Gayle let out a heavy sigh; the sound filling the room with a sense of weariness. "I'm grasping at straws here." The weight of their situation seemed to hang in the air, a palpable heaviness that made it hard to breathe. Gayle's bitter exhale cut through the silence, the sound echoing with a touch of resentment. "We both know we're on a slide. A downhill slide."

Darla could almost taste the despair in the room, a sharp tang that mirrored their crumbling relationship. She took a moment to gather her thoughts, feeling the weight of the argument settle in her chest. This was their chance to address the issues that had been festering, to let their emotions finally be heard. Emotions she hadn't really put into words. "I feel it too. I'm just not sure what to do about it."

She lit her customary after-dinner cigarette and cajoled Darla to lighten the mood by changing the subject. "There's a soiree of sorts tonight. All the big wigs. Come to the party with me."

"No. I'm not up to it."

"Darla, my darling." Gayle sighed deeply. Intuitively, she knew that would be Darla's response. She had hoped for a change, an awareness of her needs, but no. Her voice was now edged with disappointment, which seemed to signal an end to her desperation. "You are one of the most driven women I've ever met. Your success and intelligence is what drew me to you."

Darla looked at her curiously. She had not heard this tone before.

"You are … very kind …." Gayle struggled. She could not look Darla in the eye.

Oh, my God! She's breaking up with me. A small sound of surprise escaped her. "Are you breaking up with me?" she asked.

Gayle pressed her lips together firmly to ensure hesitation before she answered. "I just need more, than kindness and routine." She looked quickly at Darla with a facade of assurance. "It's not you, really!" She gasped in frustration, "Oh, well hell, it is. I love you darling," she said quickly. With transparency she added, "but you're so, so, boring." She grimaced with the last word and met Darla's stare with a pitying glance.

Darla didn't know whether to laugh hysterically, pout, or rejoice at not having to be the one to do the honors.

The dog ran back into the room and jumped against Gayle's leg until she picked it up again. "Are you terribly hurt?" She looked at Darla with concern. "Say something."

"I … I guess I had it coming," she said with resolution. "And you're right. We are dedicated to routine." But, boring? Let her have that. Darla wanted to argue it, but decided to let it go.

"I do feel like I coerced you here. Led you on." Her voice was despondent. "I owe you something, I guess."

"Oh my! The ego." She laughed with love in her voice. "Darling, you didn't coerce or force or convince me of anything. I made up my own mind to move here. Besides, I've probably been having an emotional affair for some time with Trina, to be totally transparent."

Surprise was evident on Darla's face as she looked up.

Gayle came close to Darla and placed one hand on her shoulder and one hand under her chin. She looked with compassion into her misty eyes and said, "You might think you have everything you want, but darling, you never get what you need." With exceptional tenderness, she kissed Darla on the lips. "Now, get dressed and come to the party. Let's celebrate our break up in style."

Darla nodded and smiled a small smile. She was grateful for the grace and maturity Gayle showed. She knew she had to be hurting as well, but was putting on a brave face.

"There will be lots of amazing entertainment for distraction, although a few business colleagues, Hewitt, Lancaster and what's his name? The perfume guy will be there."

"Torres?" she said, a little too hopeful.

Gayle turned her head as though to look for a cigarette in her pocket. "Yes, I suppose that's it. His last night before he leaves."

"What do you mean leaving?"

"He said something about a contract." She looked up with a pained smile. "Every time you say his name you seem a little, dare I say, lustful?"

Darla's cheeks turned a rosy shade as her heart raced, creating a sinful flush.

Gayle snorted good-naturedly. "What you need; Right in front of you." She shook her head. "Life must not be missed. Come on, darling. One more hurrah."

She spoke softly, saying, "Thank you, Gayle. I never deserved you."

"Oh bother. We were good while we needed it to be and now let's use common sense and let this end where it should before we hate each other." She took her soft attention from Darla to a quizzical stare at the pup in her arms. "What the hell are we going to do with this dog?"

They both laughed.

CHAPTER 8

"I'll take a vodka gimlet, tall."

"Oh wow! Exactly what I drink. What a surprise."

He leaned on the bar and smirked at her. "I thought I'd start with common ground and melt some of that frozen exterior you have on tonight. Which, by the way, you do look very nice."

"Well, I see your shirt is finally buttoned, so you look nice as well." Her voice held a crisp edge.

"Ouch!"

But she could see he remained unruffled. "Sorry," she said feeling remorse and a little petulant. "Still feeling wounded about the argument." She hesitated, "I worry I've lost the account."

"And I see you still haven't taken the time to look me up."

"I don't want to look you up. You're a client and I'm moving on. That's it." She stirred her lime around in her gimlet. But he noted her pout.

"So it's all about the money. Is that it?"

"Something like that."

They stood on the balcony overlooking the vibrant dance floor. The patrons swirled around, their voices blending with laughter and conversation. The aroma of food being served filled the air, mixing with the sound of clinking glasses and the occasional burst of music.

When Darla had initially arrived, she felt a pang of disappointment as she observed him surrounded by other women, their giggles and playful gestures directed towards him. He had glanced at her briefly, but then turned his attention away, igniting her frustration.

She confronted him, her voice laced with irritation. "What is it you want me to know about you, anyway? Orphaned at three, mom ran off with the milkman, brother lost in action?"

"Wow! That cold exterior of yours isn't a facade." His response was dismissive, his voice lacking sincerity. Downing his drink in one gulp, he seemed unaffected by her words.

The music changed, transitioning into a sultry Latino groove, a tango of sorts. He guided her with one hand down the carpeted stairway to the dance floor. Darla spluttered indignantly as he placed a firm hand on her shoulder, swiftly turning her to face him. Determination shone in his eyes as he made his proposition. "I'm going to dance with you tonight. And if, after this dance, you never want to see me again, I'll leave and never intrude on your life again." His intensity took her aback, leaving her standing rigid, challenged by his words.

"I don't dance," she retorted with stubbornness.

"You will tonight," he insisted, his tone unwavering. With a gentle yet forceful touch, he guided her backward, his hand firmly placed on the small of her back. Their bodies pressed together, their movements synchronized as they weaved through the crowd. Darla gasped, feeling as if she were floating on air as he effortlessly led her, teaching her the steps and rhythms with each subtle gesture.

Her conflicted emotions overshadowed the joy of dancing when she looked up at him.

His smile, gentle and knowing, caused her pride to resurface, and she couldn't hold back her frustration any longer. "Who do you think you are, coming to Florida to find me, plotting this deal, hoping to sweep me off my feet? I've told you who I am and how I am, yet you persist in trying to change me!"

Unfortunately, Darla's voice carried over the fading music, causing a few amused smiles from onlookers. It was a lover's quarrel, a tempestuous fate.

He responded earnestly, his voice barely audible as the music began to fade. "I'm not trying to change you. I just want you to give me a chance." Unbeknownst to them, the crowd had parted, creating a space for their passionate dance to take center stage.

Refusing to release her, he pulled her closer, their bodies entwined as she struggled to resist. Skillfully, he steered her away from the crowd, towards a closed wooden door, the music starting again. Swiftly, he opened the door and pushed her inside, leaving them alone to face their unresolved feelings.

The room was dimly lit, casting a faint glow on a solitary lamp. The soft green velvet curtains framed the view, creating an atmosphere of secrecy. A wave of shock washed over her as he locked the door, leaving her feeling appalled and trapped.

Taking a moment to compose herself, she spoke up, her voice filled with frustration. "Now look here! I-"

He interrupted her, "Hold on and listen to me. My God, you talk a lot. It's always about you. Always the analytical one. When to leave, who to leave with, why you're leaving." With a swift motion, he grabbed her hands, pulling them behind her back. Leaning against the door, he pressed his body against hers, exerting dominance. "I want you," he declared, his voice filled with longing. "I've wanted you since the day we met, even though you won't remember. I respect you, adore you, and I want to share my world with you if you'd just listen."

Her wrists throbbed with pain, but her anger overshadowed the discomfort. "What a pair of balls! I've already told you I'm gay, and yet you think you can seduce me with an unbuttoned shirt and some over rated perfume?" she exclaimed, inwardly acknowledging that it had worked to some extent. However, she refused to accept it, feeling cheapened by the situation.

He pressed his lips tight in a painful frown, his expression revealing a hidden truth. "I don't have a pair of balls, actually." He held her gaze before he spoke again. "I'm Trans," he confessed, shocking her into silence. Her mouth hung open in disbelief as he pulled her closer. "I'm transgender. I've undergone physical changes, but I still retain a part of my female identity and anatomy. You don't have to change who you are to be with me. I've been trying to tell you that."

Darla was breathless, her mind racing to comprehend the revelation. Suddenly, everything fell into place - the gentle demeanor, the comfort, the familiarity, and the intense desire. In a swift motion, she surrendered herself to him/her, pulling them into a passionate embrace. Darla eagerly accepted Drey's kiss, her mouth hungry for more. As his/her hand entwined in her hair, he pulled her head back, leaving her neck exposed to his/her eager mouth. Soft moans escaped their lips as he unbuttoned her blouse, each touch sending waves of pleasure through her.

Overwhelmed with anticipation, Darla's arousal grew, causing her panties to dampen. Sensing her desire, Drey skillfully hiked up her skirt, positioning her left leg around his/her waist. Their panting quickened, their focus solely on each other. Drey's eyes remained locked on Darla's face as he effortlessly ripped off her thong and inserted two fingers inside her. A moan of pleasure escaped Darla's lips, her hands gripping Drey's shoulders for support. She spread her legs wider, yearning for more intense pleasure.

Drey's thumb found her swollen clit, caressing it as his/her fingers delved deeper. Darla's body shuddered with ecstasy, her back pressed against the wall for support. With a glance, Drey checked the locked door, ensuring their privacy.

Drey knew she was close to coming and ordered her to, "Stop! Hold it in! I want you to explode." He pulled away the straps of her camisole to expose her breasts. He continued with unwavering determination, his penetrating gaze never wavering from her face as he stroked her. The cool air caused her nipples to harden, he/she lustfully stared at them with appreciation. As his lips pressed tightly against Darla's nipples, she felt a mixture of pleasure and intensity. His/her touch was both savage and soft all at the same time, a dichotomy that sent shivers down her spine. A soft cry escaped her lips as she leaned back, overcome with sensation. Reaching behind, he slipped his hands into her supple buttocks. His/her middle fingers entered into her wetness, plunging deep within her moist velvet over and over.

Darla was consumed and without restraint, let out a deep cry of ecstasy. Her knees buckled under the weight of pleasure. Drey withdrew his fingers from her pussy and placed them against her lips, silencing her cries of delight. As she tasted her own sweetness, he pulled her upright and tenderly kissed her lips, their passion intertwining again.

His/her arms enveloped her, and his tongue gently explored the entrance of her mouth, seeking and pleading for entry, which she willingly granted. Her body pressed tightly against his, every bit of her trembling. They savored the moment, reveling in the panting and pulsating of their lovemaking.

Eventually, Darla spun them around, positioning him against the door. With an impish grin, she pulled back and reached for his belt buckle, declaring, "My turn, Mr. Torres."

Drey gently but firmly grabbed her hand. "No! Not yet, tomorrow. I want to show you something."

"You've always got something to show me."

"Well, this is important. Not as important as taking you home, but-?

"Wait. Home?"

"Yes, remember? I said, someday I'm going to show you my country?"

"Drey, this is all good and amazing, but I don't know. It's all so fast!"

"Is it Gayle?"

"Partly." She felt guilt rising. "I mean we just broke up, but my job… I'm transferring soon, I just-"

"-Don't want to lose who you are."

She sighed. The moment spoiled, her orgasm dulled, Darla looked tenderly at Drey. "You are amazing. Simply amazing. I just think I need time, and I travel so much I just-."

"-Am afraid. I get it." He stepped back to tuck in his shirt. "I played my cards. I spoke to you with transparency as best I could. I can't for the life of me understand why you won't even give this a chance!"

Suddenly, the door knob turned vigorously. A sharp knock at the door caused them both to flinch.

Drey hurriedly buttoned his shirt and Darla giggled while she arranged her clothing in a flurry.

Drey smiled at her freshly fluffed hair. "I did that!" He/she bragged, then chuckled. "Everyone's going to know I just fucked the shit out of you!"

"Stop! Sssh," she said, with uncontrollable, hushed laughter.

Sharp knocks at the door again brought an impatient request. "Hello! Anyone there? I need to use the phone."

"Meet me tomorrow at the office, please." He whispered urgently. "Let me just talk with you. Let's at least set up a plan, for us. You'll see."

The door knob jiggled again harder to signal the insistence and with a nod, Drey opened the door

CHAPTER 9

Darla stepped out into the crisp night air, feeling a chill run through her. She gazed up at the inky black sky, studded with glittering stars that seemed to pierce through the darkness. The sight filled her with a newfound sense of joy. As memories of Drey flooded her mind, she could almost hear the velvety tone of their voice, feel the warmth of their hands, and sense the intensity of their lovemaking. A wave of desire washed over her, sending tremors through her body. "Down, girl," she told herself, trying to regain control. Just then, her driver pulled up, and she effortlessly slipped into the heated interior of the car, relishing in its comforting warmth. She couldn't help but wonder why Drey had suggested meeting at the office tomorrow. Perhaps it was because he had a meeting with the campaign planners, and maybe even signing a check. The thought of seeing him in front of the board members made her nervous. With his decision to no longer be just a client, things were about to change.

While asleep that night, Darla tossed and turned, her dreams haunted by memories of watching her mother sad and forlorn as she packed the family for yet another move which would boost her father's career and prevent her mother from pursuing a career of her own, maintaining friendships, or even cultivating a hobby. Darla shut down maniacal interludes of her father dressed in military blues running through shadowed hallways yelling, 'I'm the boss! I'm the boss.' Finally, at 4am she awoke in a sweat. Her head pounding.

Her slippered feet scuffed to the bathroom along the wooden floor, where she pulled aspirin from the mirrored medicine cabinet by memory. The pain didn't need a bright light to remind her of its presence. Opening the refrigerator, she considered grabbing some juice to soothe her body's trembling chill.

However, as sweat began to form on her forehead, she decided against it. Exhaustion washed over her as she made her way back to bed, her body growing weaker with each step. Collapsing onto the covers, she quickly passed out.

Her eyes strained to open against the slivered light poking through the blinds. Her body felt like it had been hit by a Mac truck, which reversed and then ran over her again by another Mac truck, this time an 18 wheeler. What was wrong? Her throat was raw. She felt nauseous. A cold chill bit deep into her bones.

What a horrible flu! Where's my phone, she queried briefly. She rolled over and found solace in more sleep.

It was dusk when she woke again. Grey light held dim the interior of her apartment. Darla felt weak as a kitten. Her bed clothes soaked in sweat, made

her feel unclean. Thoughts of a warm
shower filled her mind with necessity
and she labored out of bed. Her bare
foot stepped on her phone.

How can this thing be dead? She
plugged it in, not waiting for it to upload
before she headed for the rejuvenating
shower. Twenty minutes later, she
stripped her bed and though struggling
to maintain her strength, she managed to
put new sheets on and a few more
blankets. Her appetite dulled, she found
just enough energy to make some tea
before she curled up on the sofa to
access her newly charged phone.

SUNDAY!? Oh dear God! She had
slept for two days. Darla had missed
four calls from Drey and a message
from Gayle.

Darla quickly called Drey. No
answer. He had not left a message
either. Gayle's message stated she was
traveling home for a few weeks and
would call her when she got back. Darla

called Drey again, it went straight to voicemail. He had turned off his phone.

Saddened, Darla fell back into her chair. Was this a sign? Maybe she should just let it go. Was it just sex after all? Her haunted dreams returned to her, a vivid reminder of her mother's relationship with her dad. She didn't want to be controlled like that. She minimized the future by telling herself they were both going their separate ways anyway. Darla didn't look forward to a long distance relationship. Those never worked. *Trans!* Who would have thought? She smiled at the perfection of it. *If only you were a woman.*

She grabbed at the phone pressing the answer button wildly as it rang. "Hello!" She practically yelped, not even checking to see who it was.

With disappointment she heard Marilyn's voice at the other end. "I'm just calling to check on you. No way could you have had a hang over this bad."

"Oh." She replied in a small voice. "I guess I have the flu, not the bottle flu, but the real thing. I didn't even drink the one drink I had. I can't even believe it's Sunday!" She said, feeing alarmed.

"Yah, neither can your boss. You missed the Saturday send-off bruncheon. You know the one we always have to celebrate the big win as we send the client off?"

"Oh holy terror!"

"You sure you're okay? You don't seem like yourself."

"If this is what the walking dead feel like, I'm pretty sure I fit the category."

"I'll be right over."

True to her word, Marilyn arrived short of a half hour, masked and laden with every cold, flu and viral medication on the supermarket shelf, complete with a covid test, which proved positive.

Her eyes filling with tears, Darla whispered, "Drey-."

"What about him? He seemed pretty happy and carefree at the brunch."

"You saw him?!" Darla's voice exploded. She pulled herself upright in her chair, clothes and hair askew.

"Of course. **I**, was at the luncheon, **I** was congratulating him, **I** was giving him the bottle choices we picked out for the ad campaign."

Dara slumped back. Her pout made Marilyn's eyebrows rise in curiosity.

"Did you boink him?"

"Don't use that word."

"Oh my God! You totally boinked him." Marilyn grinned then lowered herself to the floor to sit at Darla's feet. "Tell, tell!" She said with great excitement in her voice.

"Well, for one thing…"

Marilyn's eyes widened in lustful glee.

"It's none of your business. Here's a napkin for your drool. And for another, he's not retuning my calls." She wrapped herself in an afghan and sighed. "He probably thinks I ditched him."

"Well, that is your style."

"Yes, it is. And don't think I haven't thought of it."

"Soo, that means you considered, the *other* side of it? Staying?" Her smile was wide and cheeky.

Darla's bottom lip trembled.

"Oh-MY-GOD! You like him!!!"

"I'm afraid I do. But, really? What can come of all this?" She made a sound of discontent. "I have to go back to bed. I'm exhausted."

Marilyn helped her walk carefully back to the bedroom insisting on at least fixing some chicken noodle soup before she left.

As she spoon fed her boss some tender loving care in a broth, Marilyn told her, "You aren't getting any younger. Your running away isn't getting you anywhere. Who wants to spend all that money you make on themselves? Don't you ever get tired of being lonely?"

With a defensive edge in her voice, she replied, "I'm not alone!"

"I didn't say alone. I said, lonely. There's a difference. Open up. Be willing for once in your life for love to be a safe place. Not every relationship is a cage."

"He's not what you think."

Unconcerned she said, "Who is?" She wiped at the chicken and noodles that slipped off the spoon onto Darla's

T-shirt and said, "I'll explain to
Lancaster and Hewitt what's going on.
That will get them off your back. Drey
is your problem."

Again the sad, drawn face of despair.

"Why don't you just text him"

"Tacky."

"Honestly!"

The women hugged good bye.
Marilyn readjusted her mask and headed
out the door with a, "Call me if you
need anything. Call me if you don't."

Darla managed a small laugh. "Love
you!"

"Ditto, kid!"

Kid? I'm twelve years older than
you. Her heavy lidded eyes closed to the
world.

Chapter 10

"Good morning. Rather I should say, afternoon."

"Sir, I-"

Mr. Lancaster, her boss, interrupted with a gentle upraised hand. "No need to apologize. Marilyn explained everything to us, showed us the covid test, not that we'd doubt you. We're just so glad you are doing okay, although, half that party ended up with Covid as well, nasty stuff…"

Darla watched him though her lap top screen as he continued. Their zoom meeting was the quickest, safest way to meet and organize the end of this business acquisition. It was the best Darla could do at this time in her weakened state. She struggled to find a way to bring up Drey without sounding questionable or unprofessional, when he spoke louder, interrupting her train of thought.

"I just wanted to thank you for the extra mile you went with Mr. Torres, even though he stated immediately he wasn't going to sign the contract."

"WHAT!?"

"I mean you never let on he had alternative plans. Genius, really."

Never signed the contract? What the fu-? "Sir! I can explain-."

"I can't blame him for wanting to keep the Bella Diaz name for his South American enterprises. But what you two came up with … well, it's impressive."

Darla looked and felt totally confused. Her head was beginning to pound again and her throat feel like razor blades had been pulled through her tonsils. She wasn't sure how much longer she could hang on. What was he talking about?

"Mr. Torres tried to call you. But well, I see now you were sick. I gave him your work email. I hope you don't mind. I've got the finished product right here." Mr. Lancaster fumbled around behind him and struggled to raise up a large poster board. "He said you'd want to see it."

Darla shook her head, trying to make sense of what he was saying. "Drey, uh, Mr. Torres left? What product?" And then she remembered, *I have something to show you.*

Mr. Lancaster was moving about in and out of the camera trying to set up a glossy, colored 2 x 4 advertisement board. Finally, he managed to place it in front of him, stepping back far enough so the focus of the camera allowed Darla to finally understand.

The advertising campaign picture was soft and alluring. It took Darla's breath away, but it was not the Bella Diaz portfolio she and Marilyn had designed. A soft blue background, with three D angled grey symmetrical patterns surrounded a bright silver, etched, glass bottle of geometric design. Indented facets covered its entirety with a delicate, single petal topper. The middle of the bottle held the atomizer, not on the top as most perfumes have. The spray exited through the purple petal. Lancaster explained the floral notes Darla and Drey had pieced together at the Genia gardens were the notes of this perfume.

She bit her bottom lip to still the quivering. She felt an ugly cry coming on and she didn't want to do it in front of Mr. Lancaster. What created a river of tears flowing down her cheeks was the name scrolled on the bottle. Elegant, cursive lettering in a shade of lavender spelled out-

"Mr. Lancaster!? Mr. Lancaster I-." Damn it, I put myself on mute. He didn't notice as he was talking while admiring the board.

"Mr. Lancaster? I need to get to my…I need to get to my emails.-." Her voice struggled to remain normal.

"Pretty good for 1.2 million dollars? Eh?" He laughed in a congratulatory manner. "Well, we'll send you a check for your services." He chuckled, "With a little bonus too. Come by some time when you're feeling better-."

Darla hung up the call in a panic and clicked 'leave meeting'. She rushed to open her email to see what Drey had written. Five, six emails down in the inbox she found it.

My Dearest and most beloved perfume partner! I missed you today. I missed you last night. I missed you the moment we parted Friday evening. You have been on my mind and in my thoughts since I first tasted you.

I can only assume your absence from this closure meeting today, means you have not accepted my invitation for further exploration. For that I am extremely saddened.

I thought for one moment we had connected, that we shared our souls, not just our bodies. That night was magic for me and although you do not seem to share my sentiment, I will never forget it, nor you. But as you wish, I will not darken your doorstep or enter your world ever again. I cherished our time together these last few days. I have no regrets. I wouldn't have changed anything, for the world.

Please enjoy your gift. Our collaboration means more to me than you will ever know.

Most affectionately, Drey

Darla sobbed uncontrollably. Any doubt she may have had about him/her melted away through her tears. The fears of what life may or may not be with him left like an extinguished flame from a sputtering candle. Her heart knew life without him would be unbearable. He was worth the risk. If he/she could be so brave and face life head on, so could she.

Darla brought up a reply message and adjusted her seat. She felt she had just enough energy to at least get an, 'I'm sorry,' to him. She would explain the rest when she recuperated. Her eyes squinted at the screen. A tiny message appeared on the dimming screen causing her to scream, "NO!!!"

Battery low. Power shut down in progress.

"No, No, No, No, No! Power cord. Where's my power cord?" She lunged off the couch, lap top in hand. Her eyes searched frantically through the living room. She turned toward her bedroom. That's the last place I used it. It's gotta be there.

Darla ran to the bedroom. Her wool socks hit the slick wooden floor and her body went kitty wampus like a clown on a skating rink. Her eyes popped wide as she felt her feet take flight. She landed hard with a *thwump*!

Damn this wooden floor. Whose idea was this?

She turned her head to see if anything from the waist up was broken, as that was all the energy she had at the moment to move. And there is was. The power cord, lurking under the bed. Darla scooched herself like a slinky toward the footboard. If she could just grab ahold of the metal post, she would pull herself under the bed then grab the cord. She-had-to-get-that-email-out!

Success, after some strain. Darla was panting. Her sweat was profuse. Was that knocking? At her door? The cord, get the cord. She rolled on her tummy and slid under the bed in one fell swoop. She grunted as she reached forward. The strain. She could hardly catch her breath. Her fingers struggled out, wriggling, just barely grasping the cord when she heard the knocking again. Without thinking she raised her head to shout out. That's when the back of her head hit the metal frame and she blacked out.

*   *   *

The beeping of a heart monitor caused confusion in her mind. She slowly opened her eyes to the sight of Marilyn standing at the foot of a hospital bed. She opened her mouth to say something but only a hoarse croak emanated.

Marilyn raised her hand in protest. "Ah, Ah. The doctor said no talking. Rest. You've got pneumonia, as well as recovering form covid, so you're not going anywhere for at least three days."

Her eyes bulged. With as much energy as she could muster, Darla squawked, "Get me a plane ticket to Brazil!"

CHAPTER 11

The six and a half hour flight from Miami to Teresina was surprisingly tolerable, alleviating Darla's initial fears. Despite her lingering fatigue from the hospital stay of 6 days, she remained determined to persevere and achieve her goal. She yearned for contact and reconciliation with Drey, praying that he would be willing to accept her back into his life.

The humid, tropical air enveloped her like a velvety embrace as she stepped out of the airport. It made her gasp for breath, the heavy moisture clinging to her skin like a damp blanket. The heat was more intense than Miami, but the sight more captivating. The streets were adorned with vibrant Mandacaru trees, their lush foliage casting shadows on the slender, delicate Guava trees that adorned the sidewalks. Despite its size, the city exuded a simple and enchanting beauty, blending the old-world charm of bustling markets and ancient cathedrals with the modern allure of towering skyscrapers and sleek tension bridges that spanned the brackish Parnaiba River. As her taxi weaved through the congested traffic, it suddenly veered into a narrow side street, effortlessly bypassing the usual gridlock and propelling them ahead. The vehicle navigated through quaint alleys, allowing her to soak in the sights and sounds of the journey as they ventured 11 miles outside the city to reach the Torres estate, nestled to the north of Teresina.

She didn't inform Drey of her arrival, leaving her uncertain if it was a misstep. However, the incessant ring of ignored calls and the persistent ping of unanswered emails heightened her frustration, compelling her to board a plane and directly confront him.

The villa exceeded all of her expectations. As she drove through the sprawling estate, the air was filled with the melodic chirping of tropical birds, vibrant Wingleaf Soapberry bushes, Surinam Cherry plants, and the remarkable Autograph tree, adorned with its large saucer-like white flowers with pink accents, all creating a stunning display.

Standing before the manor, she admired the architecture, trying to grasp Drey through the family vision. The barrel-shaped roof tiles radiated waves of heat, their caramel and rust tones contrasting beautifully with the white stucco walls. Wrought iron window casings added a touch of elegance to the structure. The arched doorways led to dark wooden beamed supports, while the immaculate floor shimmered with intricate patterns of red, yellow, orange, and blue tiles. Simple yet exquisite. As she stood there, her heart raced with excitement, knowing that they would finally begin the life they both desired. With a smile on her face, she quickened her pace, eager to see him and share her feelings.

She pressed the polished doorbell twice, its soft chime echoing through the grand hallway, unsure if her summons would reach someone deep within the opulent interior. A knot of anxiety tightened in her stomach as she turned, her gaze sweeping over the meticulously landscaped grounds, taking in the vibrant colors and the gentle rustle of leaves in the breeze. Inhaling deeply, she savored the crisp, clean scent of the fresh air, hoping it would calm her racing heart. As the door finally pulled open, her anticipation peaked, only to be met with a twinge of disappointment. But then, it dawned on her - of course, there would be a butler or a maid to greet her.

"Senora?"

"Hello! Is Mr. Torres here?" She could hardly still the pounding of her heart.

"Si! Senor Torres? Espere um minuto. Qual `e o sue nome?"

Right! We're in Brazil. Her mind raced back, though some of her limited Spanish, and she felt he was asking her for her name. She gave it, thinking, what harm could it bring? He motioned her into the grand foyer, where she was greeted by a symphony of vibrant colors and fragrant scents. The foyer was adorned with an array of fruit trees, their branches heavy with ripe produce, and flowering bushes that filled the air with a sweet aroma.

A towering cobalt blue water fountain, standing at a majestic 9 feet tall, caught her attention. Its unusual geometric shape created a mesmerizing cascade of water, flowing in a soothing rhythm. The curvature of the fountain reminded her of the perfume bottle Drey had dedicated to her, stirring a bittersweet ache in her heart.

Within minutes, she could sense movement amidst the lush greenery, signaling his approach. Her anticipation grew, making it difficult to catch her breath. A wide smile spread across her face, and she took a step forward, almost breaking into a run, when he emerged from around the corner. But her excitement was short-lived as she stopped abruptly. "Senor Torres!"

"Si, I am Senor Torres," he spoke softly, his eyes twinkling with a familiar light and a slight smile mirroring that of his son's. His Brazilian accent, like honey to the ears, continued, "I can see by the disappointment on your face that you are here to see my son, not the old man." He chuckled, and she nodded, afraid that speaking would only lead to tears.

"Come in, my dear. Let's have some refreshments," he gestured, waving his hand. From her peripheral vision, she caught a glimpse of a figure disappearing into the vast hallway, presumably to prepare the refreshments.

The sitting room welcomed her with its vaulted ceilings adorned with the same dark wooden beams. Pleasant wall adornments added a touch of elegance, but the focal point of the room was the exquisite, oversized furniture. Comfy armchairs beckoned her, accompanied by polished wooden and smokey glassed coffee tables. Large windows, adorned with silken, overstuffed cushions, filled the room with natural light. The air was filled with the intoxicating aroma of freshly brewed coffee and the tantalizing scent of a home-cooked meal.

As she reveled in the sights and sounds before her, the butler reappeared, this time carrying a tray of lemonade with a hint of lime juice and powdered sugar cookies. Mr. Torres lifted silver lids, revealing two steaming bowls of soup. It was then that she realized just how famished she was.

"Mr. Torres! This looks amazing, thank you so much," she exclaimed gratefully.

He waved off her gratitude, saying, "It is nothing. Anything for the friends of my son. Loyalty is hard to come by." She nodded, delicately spooning the rich and hearty soup.   The homemade taste was exquisite, filling her with a deep sense of satisfaction. Darla couldn't help but notice the drink. It was the same one she and Drey had shared at the gardens. Did his father know about her? She was amazed at how similar they acted, their hand motions, their speech, and the look of intense focus. She realized with clarity, she missed Drey.

"Mr. Torres, where is Drey? Will he be home soon?"

Mr. Torres looked up at her as he took his last bite of soup. He wiped his mouth carefully with his napkin before he spoke.

Darla wondered if he was sizing her up. He was probably asking himself; did she know about his gender? What was she up to? Thousands of questions must be zipping through his mind, yet he remained calm and collected. Speaking slowly with great consideration, he once again waved his hand and a butler arrived with two cups of the steaming fresh coffee she had smelled earlier.

"Let us go to the terrace."

As they arrived, she realized how completely drained she was and hoped she could see Drey soon before she became too fatigued to think straight.

"Tell me. How do you know my son?"

Darla respected his candor, and she matched it with her openness regarding her feelings of interest and reverence for her time with Drey in the states regarding their work.

He nodded graciously, his eyes expressing gratitude for her willingness to share. Yet, the subtle crease on his forehead hinted at a lingering curiosity, suggesting that he sensed there was an untold narrative awaiting discovery. The room was filled with an air of anticipation, the faint sound of a ticking clock adding a sense of urgency to the atmosphere. The scent of freshly brewed coffee wafted through the space, mingling with the faint aroma of tequila. She could sense his guarded demeanor, the weight of unspoken words hanging in the air, as if waiting for the right moment to be unraveled.

"Drey, is out of the country. On business."

"For the Bella Diaz campaign?" She hoped her knowledge of his home business might entice the patriarch to relax and open up.

He did not answer. Mr. Torres watched her, his face a mask of suspicion.

Actually, this pleased Darla as Mr. Torres very much must be protecting his son. He wouldn't reveal information to just anyone and if Drey wasn't public with his transition, it could destroy the family business.

Darla decided to try a different tactic and to be totally transparent.

"I have a confession."

His eyebrows raised.

"I worked with Drey on the campaign in Miami. He is…persistent when he wants something."

The old man smiled.

"He-," she hesitated, "He asked me to come here with him someday."

"And?"

"And, I was an idiot."

His face darkened. She was sure he felt Darla rejected his son based on his gender.

Darla quickly got out her phone and showed him the picture of the Darla perfume.

His smile was soft, but there was a hurt in his eyes. "It is you. You!" He looked up at her with curiosity. "Are that woman."

"That woman?"

"Drey never married. He was waiting. Hoping. I thought he was loco." He smiled apologetically for he was not serious, just concerned.

"What about falling in love?"

He came out of his lost thoughts and handed back her phone. "Date, yes. But love? No. I don't know what ever came of his infatuation from years ago." Mr. Torres got up. He walked to the bar, deciding coffee wouldn't do. He prepared two margarita glasses. Mr.

Torres continued, "No, he became entranced with a business woman from many years ago. Someone he admired. He followed her success as a measure of how life could be. He was convinced she was his soul mate, and someday, they would be married."

Darla squirmed uncomfortably in her chair. "What happened?"

Mr. Torres sighed, the sound escaping his lips like a gentle breeze. He brought the glass to his lips, savoring the rich flavors on his tongue, and smacked his lips in satisfaction. "Perfecto!" He handed the exact mixture to her, the condensation from the glass dampening her fingertips, and said mysteriously, "You tell me, Miss Weston."

* * *

Darla opened up and revealed all she had been through with Drey, with the exception of the mind blowing sex. She explained her status as a lesbian, independent nature, lone wolf style of living and her joy at finding Drey being transgender.

By the third margarita, Darla had revealed the stories of her covid mishap, knocking herself out under the bed, the hospitalization and her inability to get in touch with Drey to explain things.

Mr. Torres laughed heartily. Tears wiped from his eyes, he stated, "What do you say in the states? You can't make this shit up?" He laughed uproariously.

Darla choked on an ice cube.

As the evening gave way to night, Darla felt a wave of exhaustion washing over her. Realizing that she was on the verge of collapsing, she pleaded, "I'd better get going. I need to find a hotel."

"Nonsense! I am a lonely man, with a lonely house. Please stay the night, and we can resume our conversation tomorrow."

With his signature gesture of the hand wave, Darla obediently followed a butler up the stairs to a secluded room. Without bothering to change her clothes, she slipped under the covers and succumbed to a deep sleep almost instantly.

*   *   *

The following day, as the soft rays of the sun began to paint the sky with a rosy hue, they embarked on a journey through the picturesque countryside. Mr. Torres, with his profound knowledge, served as an exceptional tour guide, captivating her heart within minutes. As the hours passed, the landscape transformed before her eyes, revealing its enchanting beauty. Eventually, their car came to a halt near a quaint cemetery, and as they stepped out, the cool breeze whispered against her skin, providing a soothing sensation. She turned to Mr. Torres as he began to speak.

"When Drey was seven, we relocated to Teresina. At that young age, he was already aware of his transition, and it was a challenging time for him. It affected all of us, including my wife, Drey's mother, who worried about our next child experiencing the same struggles. We loved our daughter with all our hearts, but we recognized that someone as intelligent as Drey couldn't possibly be fabricating these feelings. In search of answers, we traveled to America to consult with a specialist, hoping for a cure. However, what we ultimately discovered was the importance of acceptance." He paused, his face showing the weariness of old memories as he gazed at the graves.

He walked toward a well-marked section, adorned with a pink granite headstone, Darla couldn't help but gasp. The name etched on the headstone read *Cera Alena Torres, Beloved Wife.* And right next to it, there was another grave, marked with a small stone, bearing the name *Rodelfo Eduardo Torres, Gone Too Soon.* The sight left Darla stunned.

"Did you know that Teresina has one of the highest infant mortality rates in all of Brazil?" he said, his smile filled with pain. "No, we had no idea, either," He said, his voice filled with sorrow.

"What brought you here, to this country?"

"The sugar cane fields initially, provided a good living for our family. But more importantly, we allowed Drey to finally present as the boy he truly felt he was. We couldn't do that back in our homeland. Everyone knew him as a girl, and we would have faced ostracization, or even worse, he could have been killed." His voice cracked with emotion. "I love my child."

Darla's eyes welled up with tears as she admired the man's compassion and sacrifice for his family.

"My dear wife Cera had complications during childbirth. Our second child. The baby came too fast, and unfortunately, he only lived for a week after his mother. The healthcare here was very poor," he explained, his head nodding in acceptance of her sympathy. He gently brushed off the dust and debris from both headstones and silently recited a prayer. Darla stood by his side, filled with reverence.

The ride home was silent, and Darla took in the landscape and people she viewed along the ride, knowing that this might be her last time here. It all felt so perfect, and yet, she couldn't help but think about the reason they had moved here in the first place.

"You mentioned that you moved here because people in your previous country knew about Drey and wouldn't accept him. Is he accepted here?" Darla inquired, her voice filled with concern.

"Here, no one knows about his old identity, except for his doctor. The doctor fabricated a blood disorder to ensure that Drey would never be drafted into the military," he replied.

"But I would have hoped that things would have changed by now. Couldn't he come out and live openly?"

"In our culture, we prioritize being Catholic, being Latino men, and being Portuguese, in that order. None of these allow for acceptance of being gay, lesbian, transgender, or queer. I love Drey as my son, and that's what I can give him. Anyone who becomes a part of his life must understand that this is a secret that must be kept and can never be changed. You would have to ask yourself if you could do that. Living in this country, you wouldn't be seen as a lesbian," he explained, revealing the difficult reality they faced.

Darla's world was shaken. She had no idea about the daily struggles the Torres family endured. To preserve their wealth and their life in the country they loved, they had to take whatever measures necessary to protect their family. Could she love someone unconditionally, regardless of their gender identity? Did it even matter? She realized, with a deep ache in her heart, that she was in love ... with a human being. Gender be damned.

As soon as they arrived, Darla wasted no time and hopped into a hot tub filled with soapy water, seeking relief for her tired and aching muscles. The moment allowed her to reflect on everything she had learned about the Torres family that day. She couldn't help but feel impressed by their pride, success, and their refusal to let life slip away. Didn't Gayle mention something similar not too long ago?

As Darla wrapped herself in thick towels and entered her bedroom she noticed her phone blinking. Two missed calls from Marilyn.

She's supposed to be on vacation herself, Darla mused. She hit redial and Marilyn's usual cheery voice, sounded serious over the line.

"Bet *you're* not having the time of your life."

"Well, not exactly but it has been an interesting visit. Wait, how do you-?"

"I got a little side information. Thought I better call you. It's about Drey."

"Drey? Is he okay?" Darla asked with fear rising in her voice.

"Oh, he's more than okay. He's in Canada. With Gayle."

Chapter 12

Her voice rang sharp. "With Gayle!?" Darla clenched the phone tightly as she fumed. She wondered if he was signing on with the Teen Fresh fragrance campaign in Gayle's home town.

Marilyn continued, "You may not like this. I've been looking back at old business junctures … they know each other."

So Gayle knew the truth about Drey. She had to of. Is that what she meant by, *you have what you need right in front of you*…she didn't mean herself, she meant Drey.

"Get me the first ticket available for Toronto."

    *   *   *

The taxi navigated its way along the Gardiner Expressway as rain poured down in diagonal sheets. She observed the wipers sadly swiping away the tears of rain that fell from the swollen grey clouds, which grew darker with the approaching night. The glistening lights from the street lamps illuminated the familiar path she had traveled many times before, visiting Gayle here before she moved to Miami. It felt like a lifetime ago.

The fog enveloped her and the driver as they neared Forest Hill, despite it still being late summer. The sudden temperature drop from 98 degrees in Brazil to 62 degrees in Canada sent a shiver down her spine. Nevertheless, she felt a numbness that mirrored the unemotional, concrete sidewalks she glanced at through the taxi window.

Darla allowed herself to be consumed by a sense of flatness in her mind and heart. She was both concerned and angry, though she acknowledged that her anger may not be justified. Darla realized it stemmed from fear. She had no idea what was happening, and that lack of control was unfamiliar and uncomfortable for her.

When Darla reached her destination, she glanced out the taxi window before stepping out, taking in the once-familiar scenery that held memories of happiness and excitement. However, for some reason, she now felt a sense of unease and furrowed her brow. The doorbell rang loudly, like an oversized gong, echoing through the interior. Darla shook her head, recognizing the sound as something Gayle would have for amusement. She had no idea what she was going to say or how to approach the situation. Should she ask if they were seeing each other? Why hadn't they mentioned knowing each other? Were they *boinking* each other? As Marilyn would say. The door swung open, and Darla's eyes widened in astonishment.

"Trina!"

"Hello, Darla. We were going to call you today, but Marilyn said you were already on your way."

Darla must have looked like a statue, as she remained muted, staring at Trina like she was a complete stranger. There was no point in asking her why she was here at Gayle's. That was obvious.

"Call me? Why? Is there a problem?"

She simply said, "Come in. Get out of the rain, it's freezing."

Darla's sense of reasoning brought awareness of her body, the rain, the gloom, and she felt chilled to the bone, not only because of the cold, but also because of the overwhelming sadness emanating from Trina. Something was terribly wrong, and Darla sensed it.

"I haven't heard from Gayle, or Drey," she added, knowing Trina must be aware of his presence.

She nodded. "He's at the hospital with Gayle. I just got home from there myself. I needed to sleep."

"What the hell is going on?!"

"She's at St. Michael's Hospital."

Darla's face fell.

"Covid, but…well, just get there."

Darla anxiously awaited her Uber ride, her mind filled with countless questions. What complications had arisen? Why was Drey at the hospital? What did Trina mean by saying they were about to call her? The uncertainty felt suffocating. Darla felt helpless, unsure of how to feel or what to do. This lack of control was not an emotion she easily accepted. When her ride screeched to a halt at the hospital's main entrance, Darla bolted from the vehicle and made her way to the admissions desk with determination.

In no short order, she was given directions to the ICU. The sterile corridors stretched out before her, their fluorescent lights casting eerie shadows that danced upon the faded green paint on the walls. The air felt heavy with tension, causing her breath to come in quick, shallow puffs of panic. Concerned tears welled up at the corners of her eyes, their salty sting adding to her growing unease. She approached a nurse engrossed in her paperwork.

Interrupting her with a crack in her voice, Darla managed to say, "Excuse me, I'm looking for Gayle Tremblay." Darla felt small, powerless.

"Unit 6," the nurse replied with care. "Her friends and family have been here all day. She's resting now, but you can peek in."

The mention of friends **and** family sent a quiver of fear through her. This couldn't be good. Darla made her way to the small enclosed area with haste, its glass walls, and privacy curtains shielding the unknown. As she moved forward, an intern blocked her path, his authority evident in his tone. "You'll need to don a full mask and protective gear before you enter," he stated firmly, handing her a stack of items.

A flimsy gown, plastic booties, latex gloves, a mask, and a face shield. Darla's hands trembled as she fumbled with the items, her anxiety growing more palpable with each passing moment. A small cry of despair escaped her lips, the weight of the unknown hanging ominously in the air.

Finally suited up, she stepped into the room, feeling like an alien in her own skin, unsure of what lay behind the curtain. And there she was, Gayle, a mere shell of her former self. Her skin appeared grey, drained of life, and her eyes remained closed in a deep slumber. The rhythmic symphony of the machines filled the room, the mechanical inhales and exhales of the life support system a grotesque accompaniment. Darla's gaze fell upon

Gayle's dry, flaky lips, her once radiant grey hair now dull and wiry against the pillow. The stillness surrounding her friend felt unnerving, menacing, even.

Overwhelmed by grief, Darla could no longer bear the sight and retreated from the room, tearing at the protective equipment she wore.

With her head down, tears blurring her vision, she collided forcefully with someone just entering the room. As she raised her solemn face to apologize, her hands flew to her mouth with a gasp. Uncertain of what reaction to expect, she hesitated. But in that moment, Drey simply opened his arms and scooped her into his embrace.

*   *   *

They laid together, comfortably entwined. Darla felt protected and safe. He had held her with tenderness while she cried until her heart was drained. Her dismay at missing the initial event of Gayle's hospitalization left her wounded with guilt.

Drey explained. "I visited with my dad for a few days after I couldn't reach you." He looked down at her recalling her story of chaos and laughed, shaking his head in disbelief. He quieted, then spoke with tenderness. "Gayle called and said she had a photographer lined up for the Teen Fresh fragrance campaign, and I thought, why not? I needed a distraction. I left my lap top at home. I never got your email. Shortly after I arrived, Gayle couldn't breathe well and had a horrible cough. We thought it best to get her to a hospital. Sure enough Covid, although how Trina and I never got it, I can't imagine."

He pulled away from her and looked weighted. "If only Covid was the main issue, she might make it."

"What!? What are you taking about?"

"Darla, they ran a series of standard tests when she came in and…," he spoke tenderly, "Gayle has leukemia."

"NO!" Darla cried dry tears of sorrow.

He pulled her close to soothe her. "Even if she pulls out of the Covid, her prognosis for the leukemia is two maybe three weeks at best."

"I can't believe it. This cannot be happening!!!" Her angry shrill did little to dampen her shock. "If anything, I thought those damn cigarettes would kill her." Deflated she asked with bitterness, "There's nothing to be done?"

He kissed the top of her head with solace. "I'm afraid not."

In a quiet voice, that trembled as she spoke, Darla said, "She may never wake up."

"I know."

A wail escaped her, "We might not even be able to say good-by!" Her tears flowed unhampered.

Chapter 13

The funeral was lavish as Gayle would have wanted. Pictures of her over the years with famous people from all over the world were displayed in various frames throughout the memorial chapel. Her photography of the rich and famous was renowned and there must have been at least three hundred people at her service to pay tribute to those memories. She was well loved and greatly missed.

When Drey and Darla arrived at the Miami airport a day later they were emotionally and mentally exhausted.

"I'm just going to pack a few things, then I'll be down. You sure you don't want to stay with me for a few days?"

"No. My father had some business meetings lined up for Bella Diaz and I should be there." He hesitated, "You are coming down. Right?" His voice held a note of concern. "I swear to God, Darla, if I have to hunt you down again-."

She kissed him/her lightly on the lips. "Tomorrow. Three pm flight. I'll see you at 9:30."

"I can't believe you already met my father. I wanted to do this whole, elaborate, guess who's coming to dinner, thing." He laughed.

"Well, we can do that with *my* dad." She said with some unease.

They parted with the promise of tomorrow. He on the next flight to Brazil, she, to her penthouse to put things in order, talking to Marilyn, and most important, visiting with her dad so she could tell him she loved him.

Her land line showed two messages. Both from her father. She didn't bother to listen to them. She picked up the phone and immediately called him. She felt panicked, desperate, to make a connection, before one worse thing happened.

"Hey, Dad!" Her smile flowed over the wire and he could hear it in her voice. "I wanted to check in and see how you were doing."

"Great! Almost finished with my tournament. I'll be home in a few days. Let's catch up and grab some lunch! Whad'ya say?"

Her heart sank. "I'm going to Brazil for a while." She forgot he was golfing in Tennessee for the Air Force children's charity event. She hesitated. "I'm taking some time off."

"Oh, I see. Well …" There was a quiet pause.

She felt a catch in her voice. "Daddy, I met someone." She felt a weight lift.

"Oh goodness! That's wonderful. Can't wait to meet him."

She winced.

"I'll see you when I get back, but call me, okay?" She gushed, "If something comes up, you'll call me?"

He laughed with some appreciation and a little embarrassment at her display.

"I love you, Dad. See you soon."

*   *   *

Arriving at the villa again, Darla felt it was like coming home.

Eduardo Torres met them at the door this time. His smile was big and contagious. He hugged her with affection. "Coffee or margaritas?"

"Margaritas!"

The three of them talked and laughed well into the night. At some point just before dawn, Drey yawned deeply. There was a quiet lull.

Darla shyly asked, "Would someone please, show me my room?"

Mr. Torres pulled himself from the deep recess of the burgundy velvet sofa and stated, "Drey can show you the way. I am an old man. My room is downstairs, close to the kitchen, and the bathroom."

They laughed. Drey spoke to his father in Portuguese for a moment. Mr. Torres bade Darla a good night and peaceful dreams.

She nodded to him, thanking him for his hospitality.

Darla's heart raced with excitement, her giddiness filling the air around her. This was it, just the two of them, no constraints or pressure. They had complete freedom, except for the few business meetings he had with his father in the upcoming days. As they walked together up the carpeted stairway, Darla felt a sense of liberation. She felt carefree, knowing that her time here had no barriers or limitations. She was determined to embrace each day with gratitude, without burdening their blossoming relationship with worries about the future. All she wanted was to savor the present moment. *Thank you, Gayle.*

They reached the second-floor, stopping before a dark, ornate engraved wooden door. Darla's heart sank slightly as he kissed her tenderly and whispered in her ear, "My father is very old-fashioned. This is your room." A tinge of sadness crossed Darla's face, frustration evident as he effortlessly left her side. He blew her a kiss and disappeared down the hall.

Too tired to argue, Darla entered her room with a mix of curiosity and weariness. Soft glow emanated from a set of brass lamps, casting a warm hue over the spacious bedroom. Her eyes drawn to the king-sized bed, its coverlet pulled down to reveal peach-colored satin sheets looked inviting. She saw appreciatively the soft wool throw that lay gracefully at the foot of the bed, beckoning her to sink into its warmth.

A sliver of light caught her attention, revealing a walk-in closet to her right. Darla couldn't help but feel a surge of delight at the sight of her clothes, meticulously pressed and hung, alongside a few, additional, carefully selected garments that Drey must have thought suited her. A smile played at her lips. He/she was always so thoughtful.

Darla turned toward her bed and uttered a small exclamation of surprise. There, lay Drey, in her bed with his/her arm under his head, patting the space next to him as an invitation. She could see bare shoulders and knew his taunt, firm body was naked under the covers.

"How did you-."

He held up a key. "Adjoining bathrooms!" He said with a grin.

She laughed with delight and jumped on the bed, crawling eagerly to join him.

He handed her the key.

"What do I need this for?"

"Privacy. Choice. Freedom. And don't think my father doesn't realize I'm here tonight, in your bed. But, protocol calls for a blind eye and modesty. Cultural norms."

She nodded with respect.

"Now, get in here."

In the innocent hours before dawn, their lovemaking unfolded with tenderness. His lips caressed her delicate skin, tracing a path from her wrists to her throat, kissing her ankles before grazing the sensitive inside of her thigh. Each touch elicited a whimper of urgency from her, causing him to moan in response. The heat of his/her mouth

lingered upon Darla's flesh where he
had kissed or licked her, heightening her
anticipation. Her body arched with
longing ache of excitement, a quiver of
desire coursing through her belly. He
smiled in delight.

Her hands delicately explored his
body. His/her skin felt fevered, while
the quickened rhythm of his breath
whispered his yearning for her. Leaning
over her, their lips met in a deep kiss,
pulling their bodies irresistibly closer.
As they became entwined, their desire
intensified, mingling with the salted
sweat and sweet juices of their ecstasy.

And when in that moment of
culmination, amidst the climax of their
union, Drey thought he heard a
whispered plea escape her lips, *take me.*

Chapter 14

She could smell the mingling scent of their bodies even before she opened her eyes. The musky aroma of sweat intertwined with the sweet essence of their love juices permeated the air, causing a coy smile to grace her lips. As she turned to face him, Darla noticed his half-opened eyes and the sleepy smile adorning his lips. The anticipation of their day together filled her with excitement. "Let's go on an adventure. I want to experience everything," she whispered.

Drey pulled her close, his embrace warm and inviting. "I'd love to, but we'll have to wait until after lunch," he murmured. "My father and I have meetings scheduled until at least one o'clock. Until then, you're on your own." His lips brushed tenderly against her hairline, her cheek, and then trailed down to her throat, where he lingered, leaving a trail of gentle kisses. A soft moan escaped her lips, a testament to

the pleasure he effortlessly evoked. "But
I expect you to be here, in this bed,
under these covers, in this body, later
tonight," he teased, his hand grazing her
hip as he rolled out of bed.

"This body? Not the maids?"

"Dear God! No."

She laughed lightly, her eyes
following his movements as he dressed
himself in a fresh, crisp light blue shirt
and pleated navy blue slacks. Her brow
furrowed when she noticed the snug
boxer shorts hugging his legs, provoking
thoughts about his true preferences.

"Do you ever miss wearing feminine
clothes?" She saw his hesitation.

He looked at her, his expression
slightly pensive. "I know these
questions will come, and I want you to
have all the information about my
journey. I want you to choose me as a
whole, complete person. My love for
perfumes, the pleasure I find in my

femininity, those are aspects of myself that I embrace. My analytical mind, my unwavering determination, my physically stronger muscles, those are my masculine traits. I was born with all of these. I consider myself fortunate to have the best of both worlds."

"I love your masculinity, the softness of it too, that seems ironic, but I need the feminine, the sexual gender." Darla's thoughts trailed off as if lost.

"Can't I be both?"

She brightened. "Yes! I feel like that's what I've always been after. It just seems so right with you. But, what pronoun do you prefer." She asked, already having an inkling.

"I'm comfortable with he, his, him." His eyes darkened just a little when he looked at her. "It's who I am, Darla. What I have under my belt is my business and shouldn't be anyone else's to judge." He ran his fingers through his hair, combing the curls back and away from his/her ears as he approached the mirror. Grooming himself for the day, he fixed a determined gaze upon her in the reflection.

She sensed his fear.

"I won't alter my sexual identity for anyone. And I don't want you to either. I wouldn't want you to ask me to do that. Who I love should be of no concern to anyone."

"I'm glad to hear you say that Drey. Because if you were in a flux about it, or going back and forth, it wouldn't work for me, for us."

He briskly walked back to the bed, leaning in close to her face. In a fierce whisper, he stated, "I am very secure in who I am. Besides, I don't have to agonize over trivial things like penis envy. I've never desired one. The size of my clit poses no issues in satisfying myself, or you. Am I right?"

She smiled big, "No problems here."

He sat on the edge of the bed, putting on his shoes. "Just to tie up any loose ends on this subject, as I matured and hit puberty, I never developed breasts. I didn't have to bind my chest, and I never had a period, so I never felt like I had to choose one sex over the other. However, I do receive testosterone injections once a month to prevent estrogen spikes and ensure I maintain a more masculine figure. It's not that I mind looking at a curvy figure, I just don't want to have one."

"I think I understand. Thank you for answering all my questions."

He looked at her, a bit uncertain. "I'm sure they'll be more." Adding a more lighthearted tone, he said, "Let's meet today around one. I'll have one of the grounds keepers pick you up. I have…"

Giggling with delight, she interrupted him. "I know! Something to show me."

"And by the way. Feel free to explore my room and my belongings. Anything."

"Why would I do that?"

"Don't all girlfriends look through their boyfriends' things?" He teased.

Darla laughed, playfully tossing a pillow through the air at him as he slipped through the door.

* * *

As she stepped into the steamy shower, a contented sigh escaped her lips. A blissful smile adorned her face, lifting her spirits. Darla's anticipation grew as she thought about exploring the house, the grounds, and visiting the market later in the day. She wanted to immerse herself in Drey's world, to truly understand his journey. After her refreshing shower, she entered her room and immediately noticed the neatly made bed adorned with crisp, clean sheets. This sight brought a smile to her face.

As she glanced around, her eyes fell upon a delicately draped after-bath dress, made of soft towel material with tassels adorning the underside of the arms. The dress had a comfortable ankle-to-mid-thigh split, allowing her to move freely. Darla found it effortless to style her hair and apply her makeup in this casual wrap, while she luxuriated in the tropical air that gently carried the melodious songs of birds through the open windows. Although she tried to suppress the thought, it lingered in her mind. She couldn't help but wonder if she could explore his room, peruse his belongings. It was an urge she knew she would have succumbed to eventually, so she decided to give in sooner rather than later.

The heavy adjoining door, adorned with intricate engravings, inched open with her tentative push. Inside a soft, lit room met her gaze. The familiar scent of his perfume wafted through the air, causing her to startle. However, she knew he wasn't present. Allowing her eyes to adjust to the darkness, she took in the surroundings, absorbing the various smells and taking note of the simple yet luxurious fixtures. Her gaze fell upon his clothes, and she couldn't resist the urge to touch them, to feel the fabric against her skin. As she brought the garments to her face, the fragrance of his perfume enveloped her. She was aware that he was working on another scent, and she eagerly anticipated being a part of that process.

She noticed that the key was still in the lock of his door, leading to the hallway, and realized that she wouldn't be interrupted. She hesitated as she placed her fingertips on the drawer of his dresser. "I trust him," she thought to herself. "I don't need to invade his privacy."

The memory of his mischievous grin from earlier that morning sent a tickle in her tummy. She knew he had something here that he wanted her to see. What could it be? Sex toys? Nude photos of himself? Her fingers glided along the smooth marble casing of his armoire. Casually looking around the room, her eyes landed on a glass console table on the far wall adorned with family photos. As she bent down to examine them with curiosity, she noticed a small black leather album, tied with a suede string. She recalled him saying, "Anything." With cautious anticipation, she opened the album and was taken aback. Page after page, there were pictures of Drey as a child and a teenager, along with photos of his pregnant mother and family portraits. She couldn't help but feel a sense of sadness for his loss and the hardships he must have endured, yet she admired him for never feeling sorry for himself. The album ended with several empty sleeves. Just as she was about to close the book, a few loose pictures slipped out and fell to the floor. There were seven or eight black and white professional headshots, some featuring Gayle. It was unmistakably her, although she appeared much younger in the photos. Darla knew that smile anywhere.

She brought the photos closer to her, studying them intently. In one of the pictures, a young girl with shoulder-length curly brown hair stared back at her. The striking brown eyes and determined jawline were undeniably Drey's. Darla gasped in shock. Instinctively, she turned the photo over and read the inscription: "Never give up, my darling. You are a success, just be you!" Several other pictures depicted Drey and Gayle laughing and appearing friendly. The inscriptions on those photos indicated that they were taken during a modeling campaign for the Lucky brand in Canada, back in 1992.

My God, that would have been 20 years ago. Quickly, Darla counted back in her mind. That would have made Drey 10. Gayle was the photographer on the set and Darla … the campaign manager. … '*I know you, admired you from the first moment we met, you just don't remember.*'

It was all coming perfectly clear. If I had taken the time to look him up, I would have seen the beginning of his journey, would have known he and Gayle were acquainted, and remembered our past meeting many years before. He wasn't stalking me; he had just never forgotten.

Man, I am robbing the cradle, she thought. More relieved than upset, Darla used care to place the pictures back where she found them, but knowing the moment couldn't be undone, she was determined to talk to Drey about it tonight. She went back to her suitcase and brought out the sand dollar she had found on the beach when they were together at Islandia. She placed it on the album, knowing he would see it and understand her acceptance of his past, her present, and their future.

<u>**Chapter   15**</u>

Thoughtfully, she selected a vibrant turquoise pleated, silk tank top with a mandarin collar and ruching along the waist, from her closet, feeling the smoothness of the fabric against her fingertips. This was from Drey. Pairing it with silver-colored stretch capris and turquoise Sketchers, she admired the colorful ensemble in the mirror.

As she made her way downstairs, the enticing aroma of freshly baked croissants, the rich aroma of coffee, and the sweet scent of fresh fruit greeted her. She eagerly savored the light breakfast, relishing every bite.

At the door, a driver awaited her arrival. With nimble movements, she gracefully climbed into the jeep.

"Where would you like to go this morning, Senora?" the driver asked politely.

Her eyes lit up with excitement. "Is there a fresh market place?" she inquired. The driver nodded in response, and she instructed him to take her there.

For twenty minutes, they drove in silence. The beauty of this country mesmerized her. The trees and foliage were so lush. The cleanliness of it all. She took a deep breath of the clean air. Darla thought with nostalgia about Gayle and the loyalty she showed Drey in never revealing who he was. She was instrumental in guiding him, Darla was sure, to finding his way, feeling secure, empowered. She felt a tear cascade down her check in remembrance of such a true, loving friend. *Everything you need, right in front of you.*

"Stop here, please," her voice trembled. They parked the jeep and walked to the vendor stalls.

The market was all a bustle with vendors hawking their wares, music, and food carts. She carried a basket with her, aware the driver followed close, keeping a good eye on her for protection.

Darla strolled, enjoying the experience of Teresina and its people. She stopped at a stand that sold beautiful sandals. The man wanted to barter. Her Spanish was terrible, her Portuguese worse. However, the driver swiftly intervened, mentioning the name Torres. Instantly, the vendor's demeanor changed, becoming docile and respectful. He carefully wrapped the sandals in a woven bag and handed them to her, repeatedly tipping his hand in a gesture of gratitude.

"He wants you to have these as a gift."

"Oh, no! No. I want to pay for these. What did you tell him?"

"That you were the girlfriend of Mr. Torres and that you did not know the art of sales, yet."

So, it's official, she mused. She gazed at the man and conveyed her thanks.

The driver added, "He would have found out eventually, and it would have gravely wounded him not to have known. You would have ended up with a dozen pairs of shoes."

"Why would he feel he owes me that?"

"Not you, directly. An eternal thank you to Mr. Torres." The driver was quiet for a moment while they walked on. "He paid for the hospital bill for that man's daughter to get a lifesaving operation."

Oh, yes. She remembered his father telling her the health care here was lacking. Of course, Drey would be so generous. He would never forget his mother and his lost brother. She carried on with renewed vigor.

Darla bought a few more tokens and a beautiful black willow walking stick for Senor Torres. Just before the last stall, Darla saw a woman selling large house plants and hanging baskets of flowers. Out of respect for the woman's entrepreneurial spirit, she purchased most of them. However, she carefully placed one plant to the side of the jeep to protect it from being crushed. Bowing her head, she inhaled the intoxicating fragrance of the purple and white flowers, tears of sentiment welling up in her eyes. Darla couldn't wait to see Drey and share her story with him.

"Mr. Torres called. He said he will meet you at the greenhouses. You can have a late lunch together."

"Perfect!" Her smile was big with the hope of her idea she felt would make Drey immensely happy.

The vast greenhouse enveloped Darla with its lushness, filled with endless rows of vibrant flowers, verdant plants, and peculiar tree-like species she had never encountered before. The air was thick with the intoxicating aroma of blooming vanilla plants, their sweet scent mingling with the earthy fragrance of the surrounding foliage.

As she ventured deeper into the greenhouse, natural light bathed a distant row, casting a soft glow on a beautifully set table for two. The sight of the crisp linens, sparkling crystal, and covered dishes brought a smile to her face, knowing that Drey had thoughtfully arranged this romantic surprise. Concealing her secret gift for him beneath the table, she eagerly awaited the perfect moment to reveal it, hoping he would appreciate her idea as much as she did.

Suddenly, his melodic voice broke through her thoughts, and she turned to face him, her heart fluttering at the sight of his warm smile. Their lips met in a firm, lingering kiss that left her head spinning with delight. Pulling back slightly, he tenderly nuzzled her face and planted gentle kisses along her neck, his touch sending shivers down her spine. "Did you have a good day?" he asked, his voice filled with sweetness.

"I had a truly marvelous day!" she replied, her voice brimming with joy.

"Well, we only have a few hours before my meeting with colleagues for the Bella Diaz account. I'd love to hear your input on that, by the way. But after that, tonight, I'm all yours!"

As they strolled amidst the abundance of plants, she shared stories of her day, her plans for his father's present, and an idea she had been longing to discuss with him. He listened attentively, his eyes reflecting respect and admiration.

"What do you think of Teresina?" he finally asked.

"I can now understand why you wanted to bring me here, why you chose to live here. It's beyond incredible. Your country, your estate, the philanthropic work you do, and of course, your perfume business. It's simply indescribable," she replied, her voice filled with awe.

He laughed gently and took her hand. They were walking back to the table that held their lunch of salad and marinated steak, when Drey stopped and picked up a plant with a small creamy blossom.

"Close your eyes. Now, strongly inhale and let it linger in your nose. Tell me what you think."

Darla did as she was told and she released her breath with an 'Ahh.'

"That's the vanilla strain I use in my fragrance."

"Oh yah. Heart Attack." She smiled at him, remembering her own reaction.

"I have two scents picked out for the Bella Diaz, one flora, one salt, but I need a third. I'd like you to pick it."

Darla looked at him with gratitude. "Great minds think alike. I was going to talk with you today on that very subject. First, Drey, I need you to know that I went into your room today."

He looked at her calmly. "Did you find any secrets?"

"I found the pictures of you and Gayle, from so long ago. I really had no idea."

"That's why I wanted you to look me up, so you could see who I was, at some point in time. Pique your interest in me, but you made me seduce you so…" He laughed when she elbowed him. "I thought bringing up the friendship with Gayle would be poignant, but everything went to shit on that."

Darla nodded with sadness in her eyes. "Tell me about the modeling. Why were you shifting your identity?"

He let out a deep sigh. "My father was going through a difficult time. It had been two years since my mother and brother passed away, and he was completely lost. We were facing financial struggles, and I felt the need to contribute somehow. Gayle was at the coast, photographing Brazilian models who have now become world-famous, I must add. I was there with my dad while he attended to business, and I watched these women with awe - they exuded such confidence and allure. But it was Gayle who caught my attention. She was like the cool aunt, the one who teaches you about the world and how to be both naughty and serious, yet free.”

“She noticed me watching her and called me over. She asked for my name and complimented my fine features, saying I looked like a model. I told her I didn't want to be seen as a girl. That I identified as a boy. She understood and saw that in me, assuring me that boys can also be models. Long story short, they helped me make my way to Canada for the Lucky brand campaign. However, when I arrived, they were short of two female models. They asked if I would be willing to wear a wig to fill one of those spots."

"Gayle was incredible at helping me navigate this new role. She knew the right way to approach the topic of being transgender, and she empowered me to stay strong despite encountering ignorance. I made the decision to include those pictures in the campaign, but it also solidified my understanding that presenting myself as male was what I truly valued and was willing to sacrifice for. And then, you walked in."

I was twenty then," Darla whispered, her voice laced with nostalgia. "What was it you saw in me?"

Drey's eyes scanned her face, memories flickering behind his gaze. "Strength," he murmured, his voice tinged with admiration. "Quiet confidence. You were so self-assured without the pretense. People knew you, and you didn't shy away from that."

As he spoke, the faint aroma of coffee wafted through the air, mingling with the faint scent of Darla's perfume. The room was hushed, with only the soft hum of distant conversations filtering in from outside.

"As I followed your career," Drey continued, his words filled with sincerity, "I found myself more interested in you as a woman than just a successful role model. I attended a few of your talks about gender equality and LGBTQ over the years, and I wanted to not only meet you again but find you on equal footing."

Darla's heart swelled with a mix of emotions - a heady blend of desire and affection. She wrapped her arms around him, feeling the warmth of his body against hers, and let her head rest comfortably on his shoulder.

"I admit I got a little carried away," Drey confessed, his voice tinged with vulnerability. "But, I think it was worth it. Don't you?"

"I didn't realize how lost I was until you pushed your way in. I can't imagine my life without you."

The air around them crackled with anticipation, as if the room itself held its breath. Darla's lips curved into a tender smile. Their bodies pressed together, the sensation electrifying, as if their souls were merging. She kissed him deeply, their bodies pressing tightly together. She felt his tear melt on her cheek and she opened her eyes in a smoldering passion of lust. Gently, she pushed him against a table ledge.

Their private moment was interrupted by a flicker of caution in Drey's eyes. "Darla," he said, his voice guarded, as he glanced towards the door.

A surge of confidence enveloped her, "I saw you lock it," she whispered, her voice husky with desire. "But just in case..."

With a swift movement, she swiveled him around, positioning him to face the table. If anyone were to walk in, it would appear as though he was simply engrossed in working with some plants.

Darla dropped to her knees, the cool touch of the earthen floor sending a quiver of excitement through her. Her nimble fingers rapidly undid Drey's belt buckle and unzipped his pants, letting them fall to the ground.

"Wait, we can't -." Drey's words were cut off, replaced by a gasp of pleasure as Darla's hands explored his desire.

Darla was wasting no time sliding his boxers down and pulling his groin to her hungry mouth. He let out a low groan. She heard him slap his hands on the table in front of him for support. Her fingers parted just the top of his labia, exposing the hard cherry clit. He was absolutely engorged, and with the first suck, she felt his knees quake.

In that moment, the world outside ceased to exist, and they surrendered to the intoxicating dance of their bodies, their connection deepening with every impassioned breath.

A subtle tremor passing through his body made her own sex tingle. Her lips grazed his sensitive inner skin, alternating between soft sucks and firm, short clamps of pressure. Each touch elicited a shuddering breath from him, his pleasure building with every movement.

Darla's hot breath caressed his wetness, teasing and delaying the next kiss, intensifying the ache within him. He panted in short bursts, the waves of ecstasy beginning to tickle the walls of his velvet. Suddenly, Darla's grip tightened on his butt cheeks, pulling him deeper into her mouth. She rolled her tongue across his clit in tantalizing motions, never lifting the pressure, only changing the direction.

A cry of euphoria escaped him, echoing through the room as his juices surged into Darla's mouth, leaving him breathless. "My God! Somebody call 911," he managed to gasp between breaths.

Darla couldn't help but laugh, her voice filled with satisfaction. She stood up, recomposing herself, her smile radiating vivacity. "Ready for lunch?" she asked, her tone filled with playfulness.

"Whew! What was that?" he asked, still trying to catch his breath.

"The alphabet," she replied, her voice filled with mischief.

"Seriously?" he questioned, his curlosity piqued.

She simply nodded, an impish glint in her eyes.

"What letter did you get to?" he inquired, a chuckle escaping his lips.

"G," she answered, and his laughter filled the room.

Pulling her close, he kissed her ardently, his love for her evident in every touch. "I truly love you," he whispered, his voice filled with sincerity. "You have me," his voice filled with devotion.

Her eyes brimmed with tears. "Do I?" She was amazed at how he was always so sure about her. Again, that feeling of not deserving his/her love, but wanting it so desperately. "Before it gets too late, I want to show you something." She pulled him to the table.

He relented, but not without sharing a slight look of disappointment on his face. Darla had not responded to his statement of love.

She was giddy with excitement and he looked at her with incredulity when she pulled out a covered plant from under the table.

"I know what you're thinking. Well, actually I don't know what you're thinking, but it doesn't look good. Listen! You were telling me you didn't have a third floral note for Bella Diaz. And I was thinking, a part of me, a part of you….and this, a part of Gayle. It was her favorite flower. And this heirloom blend is fantastic. Close your eyes."

His smile was small and tender as he stepped forward, closing his eyes as she bade him to. She took the cloth covering off the bloom so he could inhale steadily but deeply. He nodded in appreciation.

"I can imagine the salty, the vanilla and this, something unusual." He hesitated, trying to place it. "What is it? Almost familiar."

"Yes!" she said with excitement. "An heirloom flower people take for granted, but when you smell it, it smells like-."

"Home."

"Yes." she said dreamily.

"What is it?" He opened his eyes.

"Petunia." She laughed at the look of surprise he had on his face.

"Amazing!" He looked at her with tenderness. "My mother's as well."

"What should we call it?"

"I don't know yet. I suppose it will come."

*   *   *

That evening, Darla gave Mr. Torres his walking stick. He kissed her cheek with tenderness, and a shy smile lifted the corners of his mouth. "It is good to have a woman's loving heart in our home again." He nodded in appreciation to her.

Her smile was shy in return. Everyone retreated to their rooms, with Drey slipping in through the adjoining door.

She opened to him and allowed their bodies to press together, their mouths searching hungrily for satisfaction. The sweat glistened on her face, her forehead, her shoulders and between her legs. She never felt so complete, so ready to share herself, her life, her hopes, and dreams.

She felt the urge to climax, but waited until they would shudder together in deep moans of sensual pleasure. It didn't take long. As they lay there in the glow of their lovemaking, he murmured to her.

"I want to take you with me where ever I go, Darla. To live with me at my home in Teresina, to be my partner, my equal, travel the globe, to Antarctica if we want. I want to take you-."

"We could be like work partners and lovers."

"No. We would be partners in life, grow old together….get married."

"Married?"

"I'm in love with you." The pregnant pause lingered so long eventually she heard the deepened, regular breathing of his sleep.

She couldn't let the moment leave. It was now or never. "I love you too!" She said out loud. "Take me," she added in a whisper.

He opened his sleepy eyes. "What?"

"Take me! Everywhere. With you."

"Say it louder!" Drey commanded of her. "Say it like you mean it, not like you're afraid."

She pulled him fiercely to her. With a hundred percent confidence, she spoke, "I'm yours. Take me, just take me."

"Darla, my sweet petunia, I believe you just named our new perfume."

About The Author

Deena Kaye lives with a lot of cats, a few dogs, many plants and some very old books.

Deena also has a varied background in human services and emotional well-being training. The characters portrayed in her stories reflect real life, real feelings and authentic life choices that fill the reader with sensory pleasures, laughter and tears.

Living life, accepting what I know, changing what I can, embracing who I am, perseverates through my writings.

Always be the best you can be and love yourself regardless.

Questions and comments are welcome at BlackWillowpub@gmail.com. **A posted review from you would be greatly appreciated.**